Losing Pawns

OrangeBooks Publication

1st Floor, Rajhans Arcade, Mall Road, Kohka, Bhilai, Chhattisgarh 490020

Website: **www.orangebooks.in**

First Edition, 2023

ISBN: 978-93-5621-568-9

Price: Rs. 299.00

Printed in India

LOSING PAWNS

MANOJ EASHWA J

OrangeBooks Publication
www.orangebooks.in

Content

Chapter-1

Lenora said, "Get up! It's getting late!" "What's wrong with you? Don't I have the freedom to sleep as I wish?" said Maxson. "Look, it's your first day of college. Don't be late, especially on the first day."

"I know, I still have two more hours. I'll take care of it. Just leave me alone!" Maxson yelled. Lenora could take no more of this. She freely reached for the pillow and bed linens. Lenora hurried out of the room, saying, "Your breakfast is ready. Take care of your lunch yourself. I'm running late for work. Get ready and leave on time."

Maxson had to get ready and then cross a street with only one lane in order to catch the metro train that would transport him to the fourteen-kilometer-distance DIT University. He simply needed to travel a short distance to get to the campus after getting off the train. As soon as he stepped onto the campus, he marveled at its immense size. The campus was 200 times bigger than his school, which was appropriate given that it was a prestigious college known for its MBA program. But unlike most others, Maxson had little interest in following a conventional path of study. Because of his exceptional brilliance and distinctive viewpoint, he decided to pursue an entrepreneurial bachelor's degree. His dream was to become an entrepreneur.

When he got there, he asked how to get to the classes on entrepreneurship. Maxson made it to the classroom in the allotted five minutes before the session began. The instructor had already started interacting with every student in attendance. Maxson was pleased to see that he was in the company of sixty other students who were equally passionate about entrepreneurship. As the last student to arrive, he felt welcomed and at home with peers who had similar goals.

Maxson exclaimed as he walked into the classroom, "The Professor answered, "Yes, come in, child, and take your seat." Maxson looked around the room for a seat, and he only saw one on the row that was closest to the front. When he took a seat, Maxson noticed a girl and a boy already seated at the desk. The boy cleared a spot for Maxson to sit close to him as he got closer. "What's your name?" asked the boy. "Max," answered Maxson. The boy said, "What, Max?" Maxson answered, "No, it's Maxson." Maxson was curious about the boy’s name. The boy said, "Ax." Maxson was shocked and said, "Ax?" The boy laughed and corrected himself, saying, "No, it's Axel." Maxson liked Axel's calm and funny way of talking, so they started talking. However, the girl sitting across from Axel seemed completely absorbed in her phone and paid no attention to them. She wouldn't even respond when Axel tried to talk to her.

The class laughed as the instructor asked about the girl next to Axel, who politely declined to introduce herself with a short "no thanks." The introductions went on, with Maxson's next. Maxson learned from their classmates' introductions that a lot of them had various reasons for attending the course but that they did not particularly enjoy it.

After three-quarters of the day, lunchtime came. Maxson made the decision to go to the canteen with Axel. The girl sitting close by caught their attention, but she didn't say anything. Maxson and Axel discovered their cards were not functioning for the transaction when they were preparing to purchase fresh juices. Their attempts to make a payment were unsuccessful. The girl, who had been quietly observing, looked at it. Axel asked her in jest, "Do you speak?" She smiled and said, "Have what you want to eat. I'll cover it." After a little while, she made her offer. She inquired about their names, intrigued.

The three of them left their meal and strolled about the college, taking in all of the many activities that were going on. First, they came upon a football competition; thereafter, they witnessed singing and dancing contests. Additionally, they observed many clubs in operation, such as the NCC, rehearsing on the premises. They noticed students from different departments as they were passing by. They also looked around the event halls, library, and theater. The three of them had a great sense of togetherness and were unaware that they had gone more than half the day without going to class. They had covered nearly a third of the college, Axel said jokingly, and they should keep the rest for tomorrow. They decided to get together again tomorrow and exchanged phone numbers as the day was coming to a conclusion. Maxson took the metro train home, Presley drove her own car because she came from a wealthy family, and Axel rode his motorcycle because he came from a middle-class family.

When Maxson arrived home, he noticed Lenora's continued absence. He chose to call her, but she did not answer. After getting dressed, he switched on the television and tuned in to his favorite business and political news networks. He was so caught up in the news that he had the thought to assist his sister. Lost in contemplation, he went on to tidy the entire house. He even made Lenora an early dinner. Lenora was shocked by the condition of the house and the food that was waiting for her when she eventually made it home. She looked at Maxson in shock and said, "Did you do all this?" He defended himself by saying, "Yes, why would you doubt that?" Lenora voiced her displeasure, criticizing the dinner's quality and the house's cleanliness. As she chastised her brother, her temper erupted. Maxson justified his efforts by stating that the food was appropriate for him and that he had tried his hardest. Lenora was not impressed. Maxson, frustrated and unable to handle the bad meal, feigned to be full even though he was very hungry and had a longing for anything edible.

Lenora took the initiative to prepare a fresh dish after observing her brother's hunger and realizing her own lack of cooking skills. She made another supper and gave it to Maxson in thirty minutes. She offered him a doughnut and said it was tasty. Maxson said he was still full and declined. Lenora, on the other hand, said that she had cooked additional doughnuts for the two of them after seeing through his act. She started to say something, but Maxson interrupted, wanting to try the food. It was excellent, he thought, and they both started laughing, bringing the evening to a cheerful close.

Maxson and Presley waited for Axel to join them on campus the following day. Axel showed up a short while later, and the three of them talked until class started. After an hour, they became distracted and decided to go to a movie theater. They hurried to the parking lot when the lecturer left, with Presley driving them there in her vehicle. Presley shared her view of schooling, viewing it as more of a formality and favoring practical experience over academic learning. She asked Maxson if he was interested in attending classes, to which he replied, “I am, but I'm more interested in hands-on experiences.” Axel chimed in, saying that he wanted to do great things at this point in his life and that he saw college as an exciting journey.

They fueled their camaraderie largely through their shared interests and worldviews, rather than their academic pursuits. They made it to the cinema, but they missed the opening ten minutes of the movie. Still, they were able to follow the plot and found the film enjoyable. They then went to a restaurant for lunch before making their way back to the campus. After saying goodbye and dropping them off, Presley drove home. Axel got on his bike while Maxson asked to be dropped off at a railway station. But instead of stopping there, Axel made his way in the direction of Maxson's house. Maxson said nothing, sensing Axel's motives. After a while, Axel asked for directions to Maxson's house, and they ultimately found it. Surprising herself, Lenora opened the door and saw Axel. Lenora made coffee and snacks for them as they settled in. They talked, and the night went by quickly.

Axel's mom called to let him know what time it was. Lenora would make dinner, so Axel was told to wait. Maxson talked Axel into staying overnight as he was too exhausted to go home after supper. Axel nodded, and they found themselves on the patio, deep in discussion, while Lenora retired to bed. Axel made the decision to phone Presley in the middle of it. When she picked up the phone, Maxson asked whether she was awake. Checking the caller ID out of confusion, Presley was shocked to see that it was Axel. Maxson explained, and Presley said she would like to go with them. After they gave their consent, Presley showed up.

Lenora was shocked to see Presley there as they laughed and shared stories on the terrace throughout the following day. Grinning, Lenora greeted Presley and introduced herself. When she asked about courses, none of them said they would be there that day; they were all too tired after trips and late nights. Maxson answered, to which Lenora chastised him in a lighthearted manner. She gave them the day off but made it clear that they had to return to college the next day. Lenora had getting ready for work, so the three of them worked together to make breakfast. Axel's and Presley's parents called during this time to tell them to get back home by the evening.

Presley and Maxson worked together to make egg sandwiches for breakfast, and Axel played games close by, occasionally jumping in on the conversation. The three of them made breakfast and then sat down to eat. They had had a restless night, so they were tired and decided to take a siesta that lasted until the evening. When they awoke, they intended to stroll around Delhi's busy streets. Their means of transportation around the city was Axel's motorcycle. They strolled and talked about the approaching weekend as 7 o'clock rolled around. They enthusiastically decided to go, and they talked about going to Shimla, a beautiful place renowned for its scenic views and snow-covered landscapes. Axel and Presley were becoming excited, but Maxson was deep in thought. He considered his devotion and what he needed to do to reach his goals. Despite his inner sentiments, he remained silent about his torn feelings between his personal aspirations and his current deeds.

Presley noticed the way Maxson was acting and asked him what was on his mind. Her excitement made Maxson hesitate a little, saying he wasn't sure if what he was doing was the right thing to do. Presley and Axel persuaded him to go on the trip despite his doubts. Maxson was initially reluctant since he didn't want to disappoint his sister Lenora, who was depending on him. He thought she might become stressed out without him. But during the brief journey, Presley reassured him that she would speak with Lenora and take care of matters.

Axel persisted, which helped to convince Maxson to put aside his reservations and go on the trip.

Using Axel's bike, they returned to Maxson's house. When they got inside, they told Lenora about their travel intentions, and she gave her blessing. Lenora received 50,000 rupees each month in income. Her finances were only around 10,000 rupees a month after deducting the 10,000 rupees dwelling rent and the roughly 2.5 lakh rupee annual tuition price. But she persuaded Maxson to go, telling him that her love for her brother was more important than money. Despite his misgivings, Maxson decided to go on the journey because he knew how important his sister's happiness was. Presley and Axel were thrilled with his choice. Axel and Presley said goodbye as the final workday of the week drew near, resolving to get together the next day.

The three of them gathered the next morning, counting down the hours till their travel to Shimla and looking forward to the end of the day. But time seemed to be taking its sweet time, wearing them down. They persevered till the end of the day, despite the slow progress. Choosing to take advantage of the night, they drove off in Presley's Car with the intention of arriving in Shimla by sunrise. Presley intended to start the trip from her house, picking up Axel on the route to Maxson's house. Following her return from college, Presley quickly got dressed, said goodbye to her parents with some guidance and financial assistance, and headed out. She called Axel in route, pleading with him to make sure he was prepared and to move quickly. When she finally made it to Axel's house, she was surprised to see him ready and waiting with his bags. Now that Axel was along, they headed to Maxson's residence. When they got there, they rang the doorbell and told Maxson they were leaving in five minutes. After finishing the required inspections, Maxson called Lenora to inform her about the upcoming events and bid farewell. Now that all three of them were together, they set out on their journey, using the Google map as a guide as the car's wheels turned towards Shimla.

Presley cranked the music in the car so that it was audible during a clear conversation. Axel gasped, "You're completely different than I thought, Presley." Presley was curious, so he said, "Why? What's the reason?" Axel told her about their first college meeting and how her initial quietness made him think she was being haughty. He went on, telling how that episode in the canteen when she paid their bill had altered his perspective. "You're weird too, Axel," smiled Presley back. They were joking around in the car, and it was full of laughter.

"Guys, do you have anything to eat?" Maxson said this after Presley handed him a pack of wafers, and the three of them started talking about how they were going to explore Shimla. They were excited about the breathtaking scenery, hiking, and daring things that were in store for them. Maxson and Presley talked about their previous school experiences and how they ended up at the same college as Axel's eyelids grew heavy, and he soon fell asleep. Maxson's yawns increased as the conversation went on, until finally he fell asleep while speaking. Meanwhile, Presley had to stay awake to reach

Shimla by morning. She did this by listening to music and applying firm pressure to the accelerator. It was daybreak when the Car finally reached Shimla.

Presley yelled, "Wake up, guys! We need to find accommodation." Axel and Maxson both woke up blearily, picked up their bags, and set off to find a hotel. They realized they should have dressed warmer since the cold was biting them. "We should have bought sweaters and jackets before coming here," Axel complained. They found a woolens store quickly, hurried inside, and bought the essential winter clothing. After getting dressed, they located a room and entered. Maxson declared, "I need to sleep for a while to get rid of tiredness." "Wake me up if I sleep for more than 3 hours, and then we can start our schedule." Once they had showered, the three of them headed out to enjoy the picturesque grandeur of the surrounding mountains and natural surroundings. They started out by looking up maps on their mobile devices and getting advice from locals. They then made their way to the Ridge, a well-known and well-liked tourist spot. After parking the car, they strolled down Mall Road, which is a broad, open thoroughfare. Tourists were pouring into the area, lured by the atmosphere of a weekend retreat. Following their breakfast, they noticed that time was passing quickly, so they decided to continue exploring other places. Talking to locals, they discovered certain unique meals exclusive to Shimla. When fatigue started to set in by 11 p.m., they made the decision to end the day and intended to resume their excursions the next morning. They went back to their room and took a wellearned nap.

They were going to enjoy some snow sports the following morning, going flyboarding, paragliding, and snowboarding. They enjoyed every ride and were excited to attend an amusement park with many water attractions and roller coasters. They saw a girl nearby, who appeared to be a schoolgirl, longingly peering at the theme park as they waited in line to buy tickets. Maxson observed her and discussed it with Presley and Axel.

Chapter-2

"Hey, don't you have other companions?" Axel tried to start a conversation by asking the girl. "Are you here by yourself?" asked Presley in response. The girl didn't say anything, but her hungry glance spoke a lot.

"If it's okay with you, I can buy a ticket," Maxson said. The girl nodded, and Axel made sure she could go too by buying four tickets. Together, they all had fun on the rides. The girl accepted Presley's offer and gave her name as Martha. Martha clarified that the treat had been delayed by several months since her mother hadn't provided her with the money for the rides. She acknowledged that every evening after school, she would gaze at the theme park.

Then Martha invited us to her house, which was only a kilometer away. She mentioned that her mother was an excellent cook and had a little grocery store. She insisted that they come spend the night and eat the delectable cuisine her mother had prepared. The three accepted this nice offer without hesitation. After walking to Martha's house, she told her mother about their predicament.

Martha's mother kindly invited them to a food court and served them local specialties. However, their enjoyment was abruptly interrupted when four powerful and affluent individuals refused to pay for their food. Martha's mother informed them that they still owed around 7,000 rupees for earlier food orders. The haughty men dismissed her plea with a laugh, saying she couldn't run her business with vengeance and they would pay if they wanted to.

Enraged by their actions, Presley attempted to step in. Presley confronted the man despite Axel and Maxson's advice to the contrary. When he pulled her away, Axel lost his cool and hit the man in the face, breaking his nose. Two of the group detained Axel, and the other three surrounded him. Maxson gave Axel a chance to escape by hitting one of the soldiers, securing him. Axel and Presley made it out of the scene together.

Presley remained silent when Axel asked where Maxson was. When Maxson went to rescue Axel, she told him that two guys had followed him. She was clueless as to his whereabouts. A few hours later, Maxson gave Presley a call and asked her to use her phone to disclose their location. Concerned, Axel inquired as to Maxson's whereabouts and the events that transpired. Maxson promised to provide an explanation upon his arrival.

Maxson joined them an hour later. When Axel asked how Maxson had gotten away, he told him that it was simple for him to outrun the men pursuing him because they were older and slower. They joked about the issue, despite how serious it was. To retrieve their bags, they went back to Martha's house.

The men were looking for them all around the town, and Martha's mother begged them to leave. She told them to go back home, emphasizing that their purpose for vacation was to have fun, not to get involved in such things. Reluctantly, the three agreed and got ready to head back. They noted the satisfaction on Martha's face before they left. With a smile that radiated appreciation for their compassion, she waved them off.

The ride back was gloomy. Presley and Maxson sat in silence in the backseat, deep in concentration, while Axel operated the wheel. Maxson couldn't help but notice Martha's joyous expression after they had successfully defended her mother. At last, Axel broke the ice, telling them to get talking or else they might end up driving into a dangerous sleep. In her reflective tone, Presley stated that she thought the world was full of people who didn't care about other people and that everyone was naturally selfish. She maintained that, in the end, this selfishness resulted in dread and cowardice. In response, Axel argued that their previous experience was but a drop in the huge ocean of global problems, citing the numerous problems afflicting the globe today, ranging from societal inequities and poverty to murders and thievery. Presley elaborated on her argument, stressing that their behavior-or lack thereof-in resolving little injustices was a sign of the selfishness that kept people from taking on more significant issues. She ascribed a large portion of this to the power of politicians and money.

"Presley, you're absolutely right," Maxson conceded. One of the main things that keeps injustice and inequality alive in society is money. Even in our own communities, people frequently disregard the values of justice and humanity in favor of making snap decisions about others based only on their appearance and financial situation. They don't understand that people who are wealthier frequently treat them in an equally unfair manner as they do the underprivileged. It's an unfair pattern."

Axel interjected, saying, "It's funny how money can make people selfish. Many people dream of helping the less fortunate when they grow up and become affluent, even as youngsters, but few actually carry out their aspirations. It's a typical mental delusion."

Time flew by while they were having this in-depth chat, and before long, they were getting closer to their hometown. Before going to her own house, Presley dropped Axel and Maxson off at their separate residences. It was eleven o'clock at night.

After being dropped off at the car, Maxson searched for Lenora, but she was nowhere to be found. Despite his extensive outside and interior searches. He tried to reach her on her cell phone, but found it turned off. Maxson felt a wave of fear wash over him, but he clung to the notion that she would be back before morning. Perhaps she had to stay late at work or had additional responsibilities. Maxson went to bed thinking these things over.

Exhausted from a restless night, Maxson frantically looked for Lenora in the morning. His terror began as his worry increased. As Maxson called with anxiety, Axel and Presley hurried over to lend their assistance.

With self-blame, Maxson said, "I'm to blame for everything." I ought not to have abandoned her. What action will I take? Len, I apologize. At least I ought to have spoken with you. I'm not a very nice brother. In an attempt to reassure Maxson, Axel broke off, saying, "It's not always about you. Perhaps, similar to us, she had to travel for employment."

But Maxson was certain that something wasn't right. "No, Axel, I know my sister," he remarked. She's all about saving money and is quite cautious. I looked around the room and saw that the fan and lights were on. That's not at all like her. Additionally, her phone suffered damage beneath the chair. Maxson began to cry.

Presley proposed that they call the police, but Maxson angrily refused. "No, we can't involve the police in this," he responded. Confused, Presley exclaimed, "Maxson, who the hell are you? Do you really think this way?" "No, Presley, they won't help us," Maxson retorted.

"We have to go to her workplace," Maxson urged. Thus, the trio ran in the direction of Lenora's bookkeeping business.

Maxson nervously asked about his sister at the office. The receptionist notified them that Lenora had not been at work for the previous three days and they were unaware of her whereabouts. Dejected, they went back to their house. Presley's mother called her several times, but at first, she didn't pick up. When she eventually got back to her mother, she gave a brief explanation of their predicament and made up a tale about having to spend ten days away from home working on an online businessstarting project. Her mother required that she pay her a visit at least every two days.

Fearing for Axel's and Presley's safety, Maxson persuaded them to leave and go back to their regular lives. Enraged, Axel cried out, "Maxson, what's wrong with you? Until we locate your sister, we won't be abandoning you." After giving it some thought, Maxson suddenly barged into Presley's room, followed by Axel.

Maxson looked through a shelf for Lenora's diary. When Axel inquired about the situation, Maxson said, "Len keeps a daily journal in which she records her experiences. I'm looking into it. Maxson located the final written page quickly and read it out loud. It spoke about an unidentified caller who had called her early in the morning. Also, Lenora had seen someone following her that night, but she couldn't place his face.

The three of them felt overwhelmed with anxiety and confusion after reading the diary entry. As he sat in solitude, Maxson thought back to his talk about exercising caution with Lenora. He should have paid attention to her, he realized. After that, he rushed onto the streets and asked sellers about Lenora, but nobody was able to locate her.

After ten days, Maxson was nearly starving to death. Presley and Axel were quite worried about him. In the hopes that it would help, they made the decision to take him to a park for some fresh air. But for hours, Maxson did not say anything and did not respond.

A boy of their age contacted Maxson and volunteered to take him for a drive. At first, Maxson said no, but the boy said he might know something about Lenora. Maxson consented to accompany the child once his curiosity overcame him.

Maxson asked the child a plethora of questions in the car about his identity and how he found out about Lenora. The boy clarified that he had once seen Maxson and Lenora together on the streets, which is how he found out about their relationship. He claimed to have taken a picture of the car's license plate and witnessed Lenora being kidnapped from the terrace twelve days ago.

Maxson had mixed feelings of relief and dismay. He hurried home to notify Axel and Presley after thanking the boy for the information. They talked about the pictures and the license plate number. Maxson was starting to feel as though something from his past was returning to haunt him.

Presley asked Maxson to trust them and divulge all of his past information. Maxson agreed after he thought for a moment. No matter what obstacles stood in their way, the three of them decided to stay together until they located Lenora.

Maxson wasn't able to identify the name that Presley had managed to deduce from the car number. Overwhelmed by the danger his friends were in, Maxson recommended that they go back to their regular lives for their own safety.

Presley answered, "Axel and I will follow you closely from now on, but I understand your anxiety, Maxson. No matter what, you can count on our support." After fifteen days of Lenora's abduction, grief and despair overwhelmed the three of them.

Maxson received an unsolicited call shortly after that. When he responded, he was shocked to hear Lenora's voice on the other end. Lenora's voice implored Maxson not to come save her since their kidnappers had set up a trap. She begged him to flee and protect himself. Overwhelmed with emotion, Maxson promised her that he would always be there for her. A gruff voice cut in, saying it was Lenora and telling Maxson to meet at a certain place.

When Maxson frantically inquired about his whereabouts, the voice warned him not to follow the call. They said they would call back the next day with more information about the site. When the call ended, Maxson felt agitated and nervous. Presley suggested Maxson go, and she and Axel went after them in secrecy. They made the decision to pretend not to know each other, even in case their captors discovered they were being followed.

None of them got any sleep during the course of the night. Maxson got another anonymous phone the next evening, this time telling him to meet at the front of the Taj Hotel in Mumbai by 11 p.m. When Maxson realized he would be traveling nearly 1500 kilometers in a short period of time, he was stunned. He alerted Presley and Axel to the threat. Axel clarified that their captors might be aware that flying was the only option to get to Mumbai in time. Maxson would take the first flight, and Axel and Presley would take the next, they determined.

They rushed to the airport, all three of them. Maxson's plane took off, and he arrived at the designated spot in Mumbai on schedule. Even at eleven o'clock at night, there were cars and people all over the place where he was waiting in front of the Taj Hotel. A cab arrived next to Maxson 10 minutes later, and the driver motioned for him to get in. Though he was at a loss as to what to do, Maxson hesitated, concerned that Axel and Presley might not have arrived in time. He climbed into the vehicle.

Maxson reached the large mansion, situated about 700 meters away from the other residences and structures, in around forty-five minutes. Eight security guards surrounded the mansion, ensuring it was well guarded. The vehicle went through a garden and a lawn and came to a parking area. After that, Maxson and the driver rode the elevator to the house's fifth floor.

Presley and Axel's flight had landed late, so they hurried to the Taj Hotel to look for Maxson, but he wasn't there. Maxson sent Axel a notification with his current location and a warning not to contact, text, or come within two kilometers unless there was an emergency.

❞

Chapter-3

The chauffeur told Maxson to go inside after dropping him off outside the eerie room. Maxson entered the dimly lit room hesitantly and was greeted by a friendly voice. His eyes acclimated to the scene, and he saw a man, in a mask sitting in a silver chair, his head held high.

Maxson begged the man in the mask to free his sister, worried about her. But the masked guy said nothing, gesturing for a guard to come and haul Lenora, shackled and distraught, into Maxson's line of sight. Enraged that Maxson was pursuing her, Lenora foresaw their impending death and recalled an earlier attempt on their lives.

The man with the mask confessed that he had been hunting them down in vain until recently. He was a perfectionist, obsessed with getting rid of any trace of his past wrongdoings. In a frantic attempt to save his sister, Maxson begged for their lives, making it clear that neither he nor Lenora were a threat.

The masked man, aware of the danger he would face if Maxson revealed his identity, stood firm and refused to be persuaded. Then, in a terrifying turn of events, he pointed a gun at Lenora and demanded it. Accepting her fate, she pushed Maxson to run away and get revenge on them.

The masked man took Lenora's life brutally as the seconds passed.

After a short goodbye, Maxson held Lenora's limp body in his arms. Then he made a solemn vow of revenge to the man in the mask, Maxson ran through the building, dodging bullets from the masked man while dodging guards, and came across Axel standing watch outside the wall.

Axel, Presley, and Maxson planned an audacious escape that included a risky tree climb and a wall jump over the compound. Their haven was a waiting bus that took them out of sight, leaving the perplexed guards behind.

The bus took them several kilometers past their original stop before coming to a stop at another one. As they left, the three thought about where they would stay. Breaking the gloomy silence, Presley proposed they rent a property so they could talk about their goals in peace and quiet and not worry about anyone overhearing. After a day of looking, they found a respectable home with reasonable rent each month, which offered some stability in the midst of the mayhem.

Unable to conceal his worry, Axel queried Maxson about Lenora's whereabouts inside their New Haven. Maxson's eyes conveyed volumes, despite their pain. He exposed the gruesome reality: the man in the mask, a person without empathy, had killed Lenora. Maxson begged the masked guy to spare her life, but he snuffed it out cold.

Presley apologized and expressed sadness for not being able to help Lenora, understanding Maxson's loss. But Maxson comforted her, assuring that they must hope to remain undiscovered during his time at the masked man's hideout. With a near-rage-like passion, he resolved to take down the man wearing the mask. This was an homage to their family's sacrifices and his sincere pledge to Lenora.

Maxson described their three-pronged strategy with a fire blazing in his eyes. First and foremost, they required indepth details regarding the individual in the mask, including his history, pursuits, and relationships. Equipped with this knowledge, they may use money or power to take him apart. Axel turned to Presley and gave her a mission: to surreptitiously gather intelligence by monitoring the area surrounding the residence.

Unfazed, Presley accepted the assignment. Taking command of the situation.

As per her job, Presley set up shop at a bakery 400 meters away from the masked man's stronghold's compound wall. A car pulled in, and four people got out, carrying three big suitcases, and went to a nearby table. Their discussion, which centered on a large financial transaction of 75 crores, alluded to the stakes in their firm and the financial might of the masked man.

With a casual demeanor, Presley heard the specifics and went up to the store owner after the group had left. People informed her that the VIP in town was a businessman with government backing, vast political ties, and a reputation for being cunning and criminally inclined. Presley quickly gave Axel and Maxson this knowledge, which was a vital piece of the puzzle.

As night fell, the three of them, within their safe haven, started hatching a scheme to solve the puzzle of who the masked man was. As time went on, their determination became stronger, preparing them for a clash that would put not only their mettle to the test but also the fabric of justice itself in their pursuit of vengeance.

Maxson instructed Presley to approach the man in the mask, get up close, and capture his picture for identification purposes. The following day, Presley set up shop 200 meters away from the home, looking around for a way to sneak in. A Car with blasting music caught her attention. She grabbed the opportunity and hurled a stone at the car window, causing two boys to come after her. The watchman yelled at her to stop as she hurried inside the home. She navigated the floors unfazed.

When the boys realized they couldn't get inside the residence, they turned back to their vehicle. As she ascended higher, Presley came upon two guards attempting to stop her. She cried out, sensing danger. The man in the room heard the disturbance and decided to find out what was going on. Now in front of the man in the mask, Presley assumed the role of a scared young woman looking for help. She told a story of escaping attackers, highlighting both her vulnerability and the unfamiliarity of the city.

Impacted by Presley's request, the man decided to help her. Presley took the job as a receptionist, seeming to be grateful. Among her responsibilities were overseeing entrances and exits and scheduling appointments with the man's consent. She thanked him in spite of the strain and walked away, making sure to take a covert picture of the man.

Recalling what had happened, Presley told Axel and Maxson back at their hiding place. Presley displayed the picture as Axel complimented her quick thinking. Maxson was visibly shocked to learn that the man had planned his family's death. After the gang had methodically killed everyone but Maxson and Lenora, Maxson was now by himself.

Presley saw two people come without appointments while she worked diligently as a receptionist. and the strangers who had now been identified as threats-holding the man at gunpoint, confirming Presley's instincts. The other guards were at a loss for words.

Presley stood in a strategic position, watching through the half-open door at the drama that was developing. As the armed intruders made their intentions apparent, the mood became tense. Despite his might, the guy in the mask was suddenly vulnerable to unanticipated enemies.

❞

Chapter-4

Presley reasoned that this would be her finest opportunity to gain the person's trust and that he wouldn't let it slip away. "Sir, there's an emergency; the police want to see you," she remarked as she entered the room after giving it some thought. Presley made a show of urgency, and the gunman proceeded to look outside the door. Presley closed and locked the door as soon as the man stepped outside of it, making sure that the three of them could handle one man without any trouble. They killed him with ease by surrounding him.

The other man attempted to enter through the closed door but was unable to accomplish so. The building's security personnel shot the man and took him into a room, where he was imprisoned. After praising Presley for her foresight, the man inquired, "What was your expected gift?" "What's your name, sir?" was all she said. "I forgot to mention my name," the man added. My name is Rufus. I'm known as Ruthless Rufus, but I don't mind because that's how I do business. I have no other options. "Leave that; what do you want?" Rufus inquired once more.

"Sir, you helped me by giving me a job opportunity," stated Presley. I wish to assist you further. Please designate me as your personal secretary so that I can be of more assistance and advice. All I ask is that you consider it once and make your final decision, sir." After a minute of silence, Rufus continued, "All right, come along and join me in every meeting. Just make sure to bring the necessary documents that I ask for at each one." After expressing her gratitude to Rufus, Presley accompanied him to every meeting, acting as his personal secretary and obtaining data about the majority of his ventures. She discovered how many businesses he owned, how many of them were legitimate, and how much of an impact he had on society, politics, and business.

Over the course of four months, she gathered all of this information by closely paying attention and calculating details about his firm. She then began offering financial recommendations and stock investing guidance, which Rufus found useful in all of his decision-making. Additionally, it enabled his company to make 15% more money than usual. Rufus periodically gave her money and wealth since he didn't want to lose her. As his personal secretary and because of her intelligence, he began to believe in her and introduced her to significant members and committees.

He eventually started to counsel her and tell her before making even minor business decisions. She waited until she was fully aware of him; while Rufus disclosed the majority of his personal details, he was mindful about withholding certain details from others, including his background, wealth, investments, private conversations, and details about his family. He remained silent about these issues.

A management position became available in Rufus's recently established small manufacturing company a few days ago. He gave Presley the power to select the most qualified applicant for the position. Presley concluded that bringing Axel in at that moment would ensure the quick accomplishment of their task. She appointed Axel as manager and took care of all the legal paperwork.

Presley presented Axel to Rufus, who wanted to meet the recently hired manager. "Get moving, young man. You must be a gifted young person if Presley appointed you. "Greetings from Rufus' Empire," he chuckled. Both Presley and Axel nodded, acting as though they had never met before.

For the first two days, Rufus came to the office and gave Axel instructions on the methods and policies needed for the business to expand. After a month, Axel demonstrated to Rufus his managerial prowess by turning a tidy profit. Gradually, Rufus trusted Presley and Axel enough to give them access to his plans, illicit business information, and secret files. For Rufus, the two of them were a huge help when it came to attending conferences and meetings and making recommendations.

Axel and Presley were two of the five individuals he totally trusted. Axel learned about the illicit alcohol manufacturing that was occurring without the required paperwork and permits. It was operating profitably by giving bribes to some VIPs, elected officials, and government employees. He told Maxson when he found out. Maxson sent a formal protest to the government regarding the product's quality, along with a copy to the media. However, nothing took place. After they told Rufus about the issues and the complaint, he started to consider the identity of the unidentified complainant.

A couple of days later, they printed and dispatched some copies to the media via courier. A few declined to print it because they thought it might be phony. Nonetheless, a press outlet published the information in the newspaper because they believed it to be noteworthy because of its association with a well-known business tycoon. As anticipated, word of the news quickly spread, with individuals talking about the quality problems.

Rufus, meanwhile, was obsessed with the corporation that was producing booze without the necessary licenses. Maxson made up his mind to call Rufus after getting his number from Presley. Maxson said, "You might know me." "Who the hell are you?" In response, Rufus said "All right, so how much money do you want?" Rufus answered. I am aware of a rough figure, but you must provide me with an exact figure."

It was 1,500 crores, according to Rufus. Maxson demanded that Rufus give him 50% of the company's worth, which amounted to 750 crores, threatening to leak the information and destroy the entire company if his demand was not met. All Rufus could do was nod in agreement.

"What should I call you?" Rufus cried out. "Just name me 'Prank Man,' but don't think this is a joke since I've mailed you the necessary evidence to establish your guilt. You will receive a message with an account number an hour later. You should transfer the funds without skipping a single paisa and without delay. Maxson demanded to be credited with the full amount without fail by the start of the next day.

Rufus acted as though nothing was out of the ordinary and claimed not to be nervous about a phone call. The following day, Rufus instructed Presley to transfer the 750 crores to the bank account after receiving an email with the recipient's bank details. Presley feigned surprise at the quantity.

"Sir, could you please check that the needed quantity is accurate again? I haven't transferred such a big amount for any business, sir, and it looks enormous."

Presley, follow my instructions. You don't need to give me any advice. Got it? I want you to follow my instructions. Rufus yelled. Presley said nothing and took on the assignment.

Six hours after Presley completed the transaction, the Income Tax Division was waiting for Rufus to show up.

The groups that had collected at Rufus's office perplexed him when he arrived. Rufus gave Presley a call to find out what was going on. Presley told him, "They have come here for the transaction we made yesterday to that account I warned you about, but you refused."

"Maybe I sent that huge amount to catch those morons who demanded money and planned to catch them," the irate Rufus stated. How were they able to get away?" Rufus was perplexed. After a moment of silence, Presley responded, "The truth is, we used one of your existing accounts to send the amount yesterday for some illegal and improper transactions. This could potentially expose many of our assets as not being maintained and not paying taxes."

Presley pretended to be apologetic by saying these things, but she was actually amused. Thinking to himself, Rufus was puzzled at how the account number could have come into possession. After all, within the corporation, only a select group of his reliable associates and staff members had access to it.

Rufus received a call from the income tax officers to discuss the situation privately. They discussed how powerless they were to stop the public and media from learning about this problem. They were forced to notify the authorities of the situation for the second time. If he declined, there was another team ready to leak information to the press concerning unreported income, unreported assets, black money, and unpaid taxes.

Reclining in resignation, Rufus saw no other choice. Subsequently, the income tax department released the asset list and tax obligations to the press. After rumors about Rufus Industries began to circulate, the share price of Rufus Capital Company fell by thirty percent in just one week-the biggest reduction in the company's worth in the previous fifteen years. The escalating rumors and discoveries had caused a solid, well-established foundation to collapse.

Presley, Axel, and Maxson discussed the incident that evening. Presley chuckled and replied, "You know, Maxson, when you see Rufus's face when he finds out the truth, that he was being noticed when he transferred money to his own account..."

"Presley, Rufus might catch you within three days once he realizes you did this," Maxson said with a smirk. I'm not sure, but Axel might take up his job again. But Presley, use caution. Cut all communication and maintain your distance to prevent Rufus from quickly recognizing when he has been duped.

With a smile, Presley answered, "Max, I know." If my assumption is correct, I will likely be caught tomorrow; it won't take days. And I know full well that I did all of this for you, and that he must not find out the reality that we were acquainted."

Presley was at work the following morning when Rufus told her to come see him. There were six people in Rufus's room, including Axel, and she was confused by the strange setting as she walked in. The rest of the room started cheering as one of the guards gave Presley a piece of cake. Presley, bewildered, asked what was going on.

"I trusted you in a very short period of time, and you betrayed me," Rufus exclaimed, laughing. Tell me, who do you work for? "Sir, what are you talking about?" interrupted Presley. You have my eternal gratitude."

Rufus answered, still laughing, "You think I'm a moron? No one who knows my background is still alive. Perhaps you are spies for my new rivals in business. I've just brought you to these last meetings, and you know everything I've bought. My cell number couldn't possibly leak without you. Thus, you are at fault."

Presley said, clearing her throat, "Yes, there's no point in pretending.

I'm not going to reveal to you for whom I spy. “Goodbye, Presley," Rufus said, grinning, grabbing a revolver off the table, and pointing it in Presley's direction. We'll cross paths in hell. Axel felt nervous and scared as he got ready to fire. As Rufus prepared to execute Presley, he realized there was nothing he could do to save her, and tears filled his eyes.

But after noticing the expression in Presley's eyes, Axel could no longer stand to watch her go. "Stop!" just before he pulled the gun. The space became quiet. Axel went on, "You ought not to murder her. We won't be able to learn for whom she was spying on us if you kill her, after all. There will thus always be a secret adversary. She needs to tell the truth to us. It would be pointless to murder her."

After giving it some thought, Rufus remarked, "It makes sense."

Presley caught Rufus' eye, and he responded, "You are not the bow; you are just an arrow. "Come to an agreement. I'll let you go so you may flee and save your life if you confess and bring your boss here. If not, you'll be imprisoned and ultimately meet your demise in vain."

But Presley had no idea how to tell the truth. Then Rufus gave the order for two guards to restrain her lips and bind her hands before confining her in a chamber.

You know what you've done? Axel yelled at Maxson when he went to his room that evening. Presley's survival is in jeopardy. I regret not being able to save her."

In a frantic attempt to save face, Maxson retorted, "Presley may be smart, but Rufus is crafty and in a far stronger and unbeatable position. But I promise to save Presley no matter what happens to me, even if it means putting my own life in danger. I refuse to allow her to experience what happened to Lenora."

Rufus went to Presley's closed room the following morning and made an attempt to talk to her. Presley, though, declined to say a word. "If this is your wish, be ready to face the consequences." Rufus then admonished her, ordering the guards to switch off the electricity in the chamber, leaving it completely black. For a week, he told them to just serve one meal a day.

Rufus turned back to face Presley and stated, "I want to be kind to you. You have one week, and at the end of the seventh day, I will begin to hurt you if you don't cooperate. You'll be dead by the fifteenth day if you keep resisting for another week. I won't have enough time for you. This is something you can now avoid. You can go if you provide me with the information I need and bring the individual you wish to assist here."

Rufus said, "I'll meet you after one week," and closed the door when Presley remained silent. Presley started to sense a developing fear that she hadn't felt in a long time as the room continued to remain dark. She considered telling the truth, but it seemed pointless after all this time. She considered Maxson and the possibility that he was alive without her help. But Maxson may feel bad if she dies here, or she might live a lifetime of shame for disclosing the truth in order to save herself. She was very dubious of Rufus's statements and worried that if she told him the truth, he would kill them both.

Presley sat silently in the dark room, her own thoughts burying her as her hunger grew.

That day, Rufus announced Axel as Presley's replacement as personal secretary and accountant during the informal board meeting. Then he told the group of Presley's terrible circumstances, saying that anyone who thought of betraying him should learn from it. "I would kill them both, even if she confesses and tells the truth," He said. I have to get the truth out of her."

As Axel realized that he knew Presley personally and that he was acquainted with him, he began to experience a rising sense of worry for what might happen. Axel felt a chill run down his spine at the thought of it, realizing that their association being discovered would put them all in serious danger.

Axel listened to Rufus's comments with doubts, bad emotions, and insecurities racing through his mind. Rufus gave Axel a file and urged him to set up future initiatives and meetings. The meeting then came to an end.

Chapter-5

In the shadows, Presley thought back on her life's events and how she had ended up here. She missed her little sister and the times they had spent playing together, but she a also thought back on her family and the love they had given her. Everything was different now.

Unable to sleep in the stuffy, airless room, she wondered how this would end and whether she would manage to get out of there or if this was the end of her voyage. She sat there in grief; her thoughts heavy on her mind.

Maxson had not eaten anything since Presley vanished that day in room. He was so frustrated by Rufus's almost unstoppable might and the way he had caught Presley that it was all consuming his thoughts.

Looking at Axel, he said, "I'm going to surrender myself. I see no other options to save Presley." Axel became frustrated and responded, "Are you mad? If you surrender, both of you will die. When Rufus learns the truth that the three of us were friends, I'll be dead as well. If this is your decision, you shouldn't have sent Presley to spy on Rufus. At least we could have survived by staying hidden."

Maxson said, "I have to try to save her. I can't continue living with the guilt of having lost my friend." Reaching for his phone, he dialed Rufus, introducing himself as "Prank Man."

Maxson cut Rufus off with, "You should release her, and I'll surrender myself. But don't hurt her, and then I will give myself up." Rufus smiled and said, "I have a surprise for you."

Rufus chuckled once again, but agreed to the terms. Rufus was baffled by how Maxson knew they had Presley. "We'll meet tonight at the lakeside at midnight. Be true to your word and don't harm her." For the time being, I'll take the bargain; something went wrong, he thought to himself.

Maxson was alone himself as midnight drew near, waiting to give up and frantically looking for Presley and Rufus. At last, Rufus led Presley out of her room and into his vehicle. They all got ready to head to the address Maxson had specified, along with Axel and two guards.

Rufus asked, "You know where we're taking you?" Weakened from fasting for almost 36 hours without food or drink, Presley attempted to talk but could only produce a faint moan that escaped their ears. Rufus went on, "Good news: Your boss has agreed to surrender. You'll be going home."

Presley's anxiety grew as she thought Axel might tell Maxson the truth. She was afraid that, in the end, they would both have to deal with very bad things.

After the vehicle decelerated, all of the passengers exited the vehicle. Searching for a male, they all looked around.

From behind a bush, a voice said, "Rufus, I'm here. You should release Presley right now."

Despite their best efforts, they were unable to find the source of the voice because it was late, the area was dark, and many shrubs were blocking their view. He said, "No, you need to show your face first, and then I'll release her."

Maxson accepted the terms. Axel stood close by, nervous and afraid, feeling that something sinister was about to happen. At last, Maxson's face came out from behind the bushes.

Maxson was the same person who had plotted to undermine Rufus and maybe have him killed, so Rufus was astonished to see him. Rufus had to find out if Maxson was working alone on this or if there were other people involved as well.

But right now, there is not enough time for a thorough study. Speaking for himself, Maxson volunteered, saying, "Kill me instead of Presley. She did it all for me."

"Your time is not today. Get in the car. We have some matters to discuss," Rufus chuckled in response.

"Leave Presley alone, and I'll get in the car," Maxson cut in.

Presley stood there, too exhausted and helpless to even yell or run in her diminished state. Rufus punched her in the face just as she was about to pass out, sending her flying and hitting her head on the car's mirror. Her skull started to bleed, and she lost consciousness.

Furious and frustrated, Maxson ran to Presley's side and said, "You liar! You've deceived me once again." But the two guards shoved him into the car.

After that, Rufus turned face to Axel and gave him instructions to cross the lake and threw her away. Come to his office the next day. "She will no longer live in this condition, and even if she survives, she won't be a threat to us." As the car with Rufus, Maxson, and the guards drove away, Axel was left alone on the scene.

The two guards forced Maxson out of the car as soon as it pulled into Rufus's driveway. Maxson stood up slowly, and the guards hauled him into the home. Maxson yelled at Rufus, "Why didn't you kill me at the same place and bring me here?" out of sheer rage. said, "Don't worry, Maxson. You will meet your end tonight at the same place and time you were brought here yesterday. But the reason you're alive right now is that I want to know about the post letter you sent me yesterday before I planned to meet you yesterday."

Exasperated and perplexed, Maxson exclaimed, "What are you talking about? I didn't send you any posts."

Rufus hurled a postal letter toward Maxson. "Your time is limited-by a known person," was the message he read after picking it up. Maxson grimaced and angrily denied having anything to do with it.

Maxson demanded, "Why did you kill my family?" Maxson continued by demanding, "Why did you kill my family? What deal did you have with my father? He was a good and innocent man, and you, an animal, killed him. Why? Just tell me now!"

Maxson fell silent, realizing he might never get the answers he sought. Rufus, looking more at ease, calmly replied, "Max, I won't reveal that to anyone anymore, even though you're going to die tonight. I don't have the courage to revisit those past experiences. You can ask me anything else except the reason for killing your father."

Axel called for an ambulance since he was so nervous and didn't know what to do. It came quickly, and they were in the hospital in an hour. The medical team quickly brought Presley straight to the critical care unit.

Unable to control his feelings, Axel sobbed in front of the intensive care unit while helplessly observing Presley through the glass. He found himself in a terrible predicament, divided between the possibility that Presley would survive and Maxson's certain death at the hands of Rufus. Axel was afraid that their lives were about to fall apart and that Rufus would take over permanently.

Axel was standing there, sobbing for what appeared to be their impending demise, when he discovered that Rufus had missed three calls asking to make sure Presley was dead.

Axel didn't answer the phone since, in his opinion, it wasn't the appropriate moment. After some time passed, Rufus gave the order for the guards to bring Maxson to the lakeside-the same location where Presley's events the day before had taken place.

Maxson, Rufus, and the two guards made their way to the lakefront. Rufus shoved Maxson out of the car and forced him to kneel; Maxson, weak and fatigued from not eating all day, was defenseless. Rufus aimed a gun at Maxson. Maxson knelt and accepted that this was his last day on Earth, feeling exhausted and unable to move rapidly. His sister, Presley, and his family had all vanished. He was thinking, "I'm sorry, Presley. I should have saved you, even if it meant sacrificing myself, but I failed."

Maxson closed his eyes, bracing himself for his impending death as these ideas weighed heavily on his mind. Through the darkness came the sound of gunfire.

Rufus's shoulder was spurting blood as he yelled in agony, startling the guards amid the confusion. The guards were confused because they could see no one close when he dropped his rifle. Another gun went off, shooting one of the guards' dead and causing him to fall to the ground. Fear paralyzed Rufus and the surviving guard.

Roughly in his twenties, a young man emerged from the woods. When the guard saw him, he made an attempt to fight him. The young man defended himself, and the guard traded blows; then the young man attacked. The young man realized he couldn't beat the guard and tried to shoot him twice, but failed. The guard kicked the revolver out of his grasp during the scuffle.

The guard was obviously stronger than the other, and the struggle went on. They went on fighting, but Rufus, in excruciating pain, went to the car for first aid materials. He dressed his wound with bandages and some medication, but the pain was too much for him to handle. He begged a security officer to hurry up. "You moron, we can deal with him later. I'm bleeding and can't bear this anymore. It feels like I'm in hell. Come quickly and drive me to the hospital!"

The guard ran to the car, giving up the battle. The guard struggled to get inside the car and drove off when the young man refused to let him take it.

Maxson started to lose consciousness as he lay on the ground, too weak to move. He lay there helpless to do anything while he heard screaming, gunfire, and fighting. The young man who had fought the guard turned to face the leaving car and eventually left the area, not even seeming to care about Maxson's state.

Maxson was too weak to move, so he spent the entire night lying on the ground. He slowly mustered the strength to stand and stroll as the first rays of the morning sun warmed his face. He navigated the streets until he came to a busy traffic area in the city.

His physical state was still weak, though, and he felled down in the middle of the road. Concerned by what was happening, a crowd rapidly gathered around him. An old man in the crowd spritzed Maxson with water and offered him a drink. Maxson came to somewhat of a consciousness again, though he was too weak to complain.

Rather, he made an urgent request for a cell phone from the throng. One of the onlookers gave him a cell phone to use.

When Maxson called Axel on his cell phone, Axel responded with a mixture of surprise and happiness. Maxson introduced himself, and Axel, obviously overjoyed, asked him where he was and how he got out.

But Maxson interrupted Axel's questioning to inquire as to where they were now.

After giving the address of the hospital to Maxson, Axel asked, "Where are you, and what happened to you? I'll come to you and explain everything." Maxson then gave the phone back to its owner and began running toward the hospital, which was roughly three miles away from where he was currently.

Back at his house, top medical professionals were treating Rufus for his injured shoulder. He had not seen and still did not know who the young man was who had tried to kill him the night before. But Rufus was positive that this was the person who had followed him that evening and had written him the foreboding letter. He knew he had to find and kill this man because he regarded him as a possible threat. The young man's near-fatal shot at Rufus's shoulder demonstrated his unpredictable nature.

Rufus was also worried about Maxson, Presley, and Axel and their locations. Axel had not given him any information either. Rufus pondered these ideas while adhering to the physician's recommendations to stay in bed, not raise any weight, and wait for at least 15 days for his wound to heal.

As soon as Maxson got to the hospital, he went looking for Axel. Maxson's condition shocked Axel when he saw the bleeding, little cuts, and general frailty. For appropriate care, he pleaded with Maxson to check himself into a hospital.

Maxson, however, declined, saying he wished to meet Presley. He was determined to protect her since he felt guilty about entangling her in his problems. He asked if he might have a conversation with her. Presley was showing some encouraging indications of recovery, Axel added, and the doctors had advised they talk to her in the evening. It would have to wait until then for Maxson.

Maxson hadn't eaten in three days, so Axel brought him some food. Maxson was so hungry that he ate the entire dish in the hopes that Presley would recover. After telling Maxson about how he had brought Presley to the hospital, Axel went on to question him about his own escape and adventures.

Maxson clarified that he lost consciousness and was unaware of what had occurred to him. He claimed to have heard three gunshots and the noises of a struggle, which seemed to indicate that someone had come to his aid even if it didn't appear to be their goal. Since the person who had aided him had not offered him any further support and had simply departed the scene, Maxson surmised that the person may have been an enemy of those he was with. Maxson thought that God had come to his aid in the guise of a stranger.

The physicians approved Maxson and Axel's brief visitation with Presley in the evening. Anxiously, they went into her hospital room.

Reunited with Axel and Maxson, Presley grinned. Maxson gave Presley a hug and said he was sorry for everything he had done to her. Presley comforted Maxson, telling him she was just happy to see them all alive and that she had never questioned his friendship.

Maxson requested that Presley swear to return to her hometown after she healed, as it was no longer safe for her. She requested Maxson accompany her and said yes. But Maxson's plans were different. He couldn't go until he had defeated Rufus because he was that committed to it. He was afraid for Presley and Axel's safety and didn't want to involve them anymore.

Maxson and Axel got into a furious debate, and both gave their side of the story. In the end, Maxson decided that Axel may help but not directly participate in any risky activities. He made Axel swear that if something were to happen to him, Axel had to put his own safety first and refrain from attempting to save him. Axel accepted this agreement.

The three buddies started making plans for their uncertain future after deciding on their roles and wishing for a safe and successful outcome to the trials that lay ahead.

Maxson took some time to think over Presley's request. Given all they had gone through together, he knew he could trust her and Axel. He made the decision that it was time to tell Rufus about his background and their relationship.

Maxson began to open up, saying, "Presley, there are things I haven't told you, things about my past and the connection between me and Rufus. It all started with my father, who was involved in some dangerous activities. He had crossed paths with Rufus, who wanted something from him. I'm not sure what that was, but my father refused to comply."

He went on, "Rufus didn't take kindly to the refusal. He had my father killed, and that's when everything changed for me. I've been seeking revenge and justice ever since. My journey to bring Rufus down and expose his illegal activities has been long and challenging, but I can't stop now. Lenora's death, my family's tragedy-it all ties back to him."

Taking a deep breath, Maxson met Presley's gaze and revealed a side of himself that he had long since kept buried.

Chapter-6

Maxson started to narrate what had happened seven years prior. "While I'm not sure why Rufus specifically targeted my family, I will tell you what I saw and remembered. We were both residents of the same state at the time. My mother, father, sister Lenora, and older brother Merrick made up our family. Both Merrick and Lenora were attending college. My mother was a stay-at-home mom, and I was the youngest in the family. Regarding my father, I was largely ignorant of his profession. Even from us, he never revealed where he got his money from. He was a truly amazing individual who was courteous and very respectful. He had more secrets than anyone could know.

"My father was incredibly kind and met all of our family's needs. At home, he answered many calls, but he never did so in front of us. He was a mysterious person. My sister Lenora was a kind and kind girl who loved all of us in the family. My older brother, Merrick, meanwhile, came across as more dubious. He was an observant and perceptive man who hardly spoke. He possessed a special talent for reading people's body language and the eyesight to determine their feelings. To the best of my memory, Merrick had never wept and showed no signs of weakness. He never revealed the whole amount of his knowledge, but I have a suspicion that he knew something about our father.

"I bring up my father a lot because it was because of him that our family's sorrow started. One evening, as we were all seated in the dining hall enjoying our meal, there was a knock on the door. When I replied, Rufus and two of his soldiers stormed into our house, much to our horror. My father requested everyone to leave and insisted on having a private conversation with Rufus. But Rufus made it plain that he wasn't there to have a discussion. Rather, he said it was an order to execute my father, saying he had no other option and that he would die if he didn't follow through. My father offered himself to Rufus, pleading with him not to hurt his family, in an act of selflessness.

"Rufus gestured to his guards, who immediately put my father to death. He collapsed on the floor, dead. The guards killed my mother and my brother Merrick in a horrible series of events that ensued. Lenora and I escaped, racing for miles, as they turned their rifles on me. They came after us, but fortunately we were able to avoid them for the time being.

"It's still unclear why Rufus chose to target my father and our family. I've tried asking Rufus questions, but he's never really opened up. I'm committed to solving the mysteries surrounding my father and learning the real story behind his execution. I have to finish this before I can be at rest."

Axel and Presley listened in quiet as Maxson wrapped up his tale, clearly touched by the terrible turn of events that had occurred in Maxson's life.

Maxson asked Axel to call Rufus. When Rufus picked up the phone, Axel yelled, "Where have you been, you idiot? I've been attempting to contact you for a very long time." Axel clarified, "Sir, I had an accident, but I was just let go." Saying, "Never mind that; I didn't ask," Rufus broke off. Let's discuss Presley's predicament." To which Axel answered, "She's dead, sir."

Then Rufus told Axel about the incident with his wound, Maxson's uncertain future, and the unidentified boy who had interrupted their plans. Axel hung up the phone after telling Rufus he would see him tomorrow.

"That moron got shot by the stranger who saved you unintentionally," Axel grinned and said to Maxson. "There must be someone else waiting to seek revenge against Rufus," Maxson replied with a smirk. We share an adversary. To express my gratitude for all that he has done for me, I wish we could get together again."

Rufus argued with nurses and doctors to be released from their positions due to several business meetings and initiatives. With threats hanging over him, he didn't see the purpose of taking a break at the hospital. After a lengthy discussion, they sent him home and released him.

After three days, Presley was well enough to go back home. She had been looking forward to seeing her folks again for months. At the station, Axel and Maxson were waiting for a train to take Presley away. The train came as the three were talking. Axel and Maxson waved to Presley as she left, and Maxson told her, "We'll meet again soon." The train pulled away.

"We need to find the boy who threatened Rufus and join forces with him," Maxson said, turning to face Axel. We can easily overcome Rufus with his assistance." Axel let out a big laugh. "I'm not joking, Axel; it's a serious matter," declared a gravely serious Maxson. Then Axel displayed a picture and a message that Rufus had sent him. It was a note on a post cover that said, "You managed to get away the last time, but not this time. The allotted time will expire in two days." Rufus requested that Axel track down and kill this boy in his letter. "We can find this boy by tracking Rufus," Axel said to Maxson. How will we locate Rufus if he hides out of his residence for two days due to fear?" "Rufus is not one to fear; he is an egomaniac," Axel retorted. He's obviously searching for the youngster because he's swift and determined to get rid of him." Then Maxson proposed, "Our mission is straightforward. For the next 48 hours, we have to go where Rufus goes. We can find clues to locate that boy by following him around."

In order to keep Rufus from spotting them, Axel and Maxson rented a car and set out to follow him from a safe distance the following day. They searched everywhere for the boy who had threatened Rufus, but they couldn't find him. Axel and Maxson followed Rufus as he went to different hotels, apartments, and workplace meetings for business.

Maxson couldn't help but wonder, As another day passed without any evidence of the boy trailing Rufus, Maxson couldn't help but wonder if the letter was fake and only written to threaten Rufus. Exasperated, Axel retorted, "Maxson, stop. Avoid overanalyzing it. That night, the boy summoned the bravery to face him. He seemed courageous. We ought to hold off till he arrives."

They parked their vehicles a short distance away, waited the whole night, and even slept there. The car that belonged to Rufus left his residence early the next morning and drove toward the main road. Axel drove their Car, following Rufus, who was rather dazed. The day faded into the evening as night descended and the stars began to twinkle in the sky. With three guards in tow, Rufus was heading home as night fell. Still, no one had materialized.

Maxson was left wondering, "What's happening?" as the two days were drawing to a conclusion. Why aren't people attending?" Only a few kilometers separated them from Rufus's home, and they were traveling on an empty road with only Maxson's car in the distance and Rufus's car as the only passing vehicles.

Maxson and Axel observed everything from their parked automobile a few meters behind Rufus's

A young man pulled his car to a halt opposite Rufus' vehicle. Accompanied by two others, he confidently approached Rufus, brandishing firearms. Panic and fear gripped Rufus as he recognized the assailant.

"You're the one who tried to kill me that day! Why are you doing this? Who are you? Tell me, and I'll compensate you. Let me live!" Rufus pleaded desperately; his words tinged with desperation.

With only one guard standing between Rufus and the impending danger, the young man effortlessly neutralized him. Rufus, now defenseless, began to stammer and babble incoherently. The assailant, however, merely smiled, relishing the terror he instilled.

"Letting you die with a question is better than telling you the truth," stated the kid.

Rufus felt frightened. The boy refused to accept his plea, telling him, "I just sent you a letter that your time is limited."

The boy proceeded to shoot Rufus in the head. Rufus perished after tumbling to the ground.

Maxson was shocked to see the youngster who had murdered Rufus in front of him. The child Maxson had made an unsuccessful attempt to subdue Who is this man?

After dragging Rufus and the three guards into their automobile, the two men set fire to the entire vehicle. When they finished, the boy noticed an automobile watching them from a distance. After muttering something to the two men, they all sprinted in the direction of Maxson's automobile and pointed firearms at him.

The boy came up to Axel and Maxson. "Who are the two of you? "Exit the vehicle," he commanded.

Scared and nervous, Maxson and Axel began to talk nonstop. They were much more afraid when the boy threatened to kill them. "We're not his allies!" cried Maxson. We're coming to exact revenge on him for our treatment!

Maxson told the boy everything out of terror. "He killed my family," sobbed. "Please don't hurt us."

After dropping his rifle, the man gave Maxson a hug. "Maxson, why didn't you tell me this earlier?" he responded. "I'm very glad you're still here. Have you been somewhere? I believed you to be deceased."

Maxson felt surprised. He said, "Do you know me?" "Have we previously met? I'm not sure how you found out my name."

"I'm Merrick, your sibling," the young man answered.

Maxson let out a happy cry. He was at a loss for how to communicate his emotions. Axel also felt taken aback.

Maxson stated, "We witnessed Rufus shoot every member of our family." "I saw him shoot you too."

Merrick grinned. "Not exactly," he responded. "I feigned to be dead, but they shot me above the chest. After that, I received care and grew better."

Merrick remarked, "I saw them chasing after Lenora and you." "Whatever became of Lenora? Is she still alive?"

Maxson was quiet for a while. Then he continued, "Yeah, but before we met Rufus, he managed to identify us, track us down, and murder her. Twice I got away from him, one of them the night you came to my rescue."

Merrick was apologetic. "I should have killed him earlier," he stated. "I was too late."

"Be at ease," Maxson reassured. "Our threat is no longer present. Nobody remains to pose a threat to us. Finally, we are able to live in peace."

Merrick let out a loud laugh. "Do you think killing Rufus is the end of it?" he asked. "Rufus merely served as a puppet. The actual game is about to begin.

Chapter-7

The news of Rufus's passing quickly gained traction, taking over social media and Television. As individuals attempted to put together the events leading up to his tragic demise, speculation abounded. The next day, experts and analysts discussed the possible motives and suspects for Rufus's death, making it the subject of every news channel.

The police established a speciall investigation unit under intense pressure to crack the case and figure out why Rufus was killed. Rufus's mysterious past and the lack of obvious leads heightened the mystery. The government intervened to seize custody of his enormous fortune because there was no recognized family or heir to contest his possessions.

A recording supplied to media outlets and played during a live news broadcast caused shockwaves across the country. A disembodied voice said, "I killed Rufus, but he was no noble man," claiming to be the cause of Rufus's demise. He was a murderer, a robber, and a cheat. Next week, all of your additional questions will have their answers disclosed. Watch this space for updates."

The terrifying message left the public reeling, their minds buzzing with questions and a sense of unease. The expectation of such disclosures only added to the suspense and fear surrounding Rufus's passing. The countdown to next week's program started as the country held its breath simultaneously.

Maxson couldn't resist asking the two men who had accompanied Merrick who they were and where they were going when they dropped him off at his house. The evercryptic Merrick just answered, "They will be here when we need them."

Maxson inquired about Merrick's living situation in the mansion out of curiosity. Merrick's answer was succinct but impactful: "Yes, up until yesterday. We three will be together for the time being."

The three of them gathered around the television when they got inside because they were interested in a recording that was on. "I killed Rufus, but he was no noble man," a disembodied voice said as Merrick watched in a mix of shock and uncertainty. He was a murderer, a robber, and a cheat. Next week, all of your additional questions will have their answers disclosed. Watch this space for updates."

Maxson looked at Merrick, and his eyes widened in shock. With a hint of fear in his voice, he questioned, "Did that mean you?"

With an incomprehensible face, Merrick shook his head. He said warily, "I don't have any idea about that." "But I'm aware that there are a lot of traps and setbacks ahead until I accomplish this mission."

Maxson had an insatiable curiosity. His tone was urgent as he said, "What mission?"

Merrick made a vague but insightful remark. He stated, "We just climbed the first step of a mountain," with a tinge of resolve in his voice. "There are a lot of things I have to do for our father's wish."

Maxson became really irritated. With a frustrated tone, he asked, "What are you hiding from me?" "Break the suspense and mystery around you!"

Merrick held his ground, his eyes unblinking. "It's not right now," he argued. "When the moment is right, you'll know it. I'm sorry, Maxson. You will achieve nothing until you are prepared to reveal your true self. Anything is possible. Prepare yourself for the fallout."

Maxson's thoughts whirled, trying to process the significance of Merrick's remarks. He was aware that Merrick was not what he seemed and that there was a dangerous and covert hidden motive. There were dangerous curves and twists on the way ahead. Maxson could not get rid of the notion that he had just made a decisive step into the unknown as he prepared himself for the inevitable outcomes.

Merrick thanked Axel for his steadfast assistance and devotion during their expedition. Axel had shown invaluable service in helping Merrick's brother in times of need and was determined to protect Merrick until he was safe.

Maxson's phone rang as the three of them were getting ready for dinner. He was delighted to see the Presley's and said, "Hey, Max! What's up with you? How is Axel faring?"

Presley expressed her incredulity and curiosity about the events and inquired about the televised tape. When will they be going home? she inquired as well.

Remaining stunned by the latest information, Maxson described the startling sequence of events that had taken place. With a tone of incredulity, he said, "You won't believe what I'm about to say." "I feared Rufus, but I was even more terrified when I witnessed a young man assassinate him."

Presley's curiosity piqued. "Who?" he inquired; his tone loaded with curiosity.

The shocking revelation came from Maxson: "It was my brother, Merrick."

Presley flinched back in dismay. "What?" she cried out. "Is he still living? Yet you claimed he was deceased to me."

Maxson gave a nod of agreement. He said, "I was wrong, but I thought so too."

Presley cautioned them, worried about their safety. He said, "Be careful and stay safe," and hung up the phone.

Maxson felt the weight of the revelation pressing hard against his thoughts. He was shocked to learn that his brother had contributed to Rufus's demise, and their future seemed uncertain as a result. Maxson realized that they would need to exercise caution to escape the dangers that awaited them as they started the next leg of their adventure.

Merrick showed Maxson a picture of the man they planned to abduct the following day. He gave Axel and Maxson instructions to follow the man attentively and to be ready. Was this the man they were going after? Maxson questioned. After saying earlier that this was a massive network and that this man was the one giving commands to Rufus, Merrick became agitated and yelled. He warned them to exercise caution and said that this individual might be able to save them time.

Axel followed the man on a motorcycle the following morning, while Merrick and Maxson followed him in a sedan. After parking his car in a designated place, the man proceeded to the retail mall. They all three waited for the man to get back in his car.

The man returned to the parking lot a few hours later. Merrick put his hand behind the man's shoulder. Merrick struck the man firmly in the face as he turned his face back. The man started to protect himself as his face grew larger. Then Maxson and Axel got involved, beating the man until he passed out. After that, they got him into Merrick's vehicle and returned to his home.

Merrick had pulled off a successful operation, and he now held the man they were after. He was aware that there were still many obstacles to overcome and that this was only the start of their endeavor. But he knew he had the perfect group behind him to see his vision through.

Seated in tight silence, Merrick and the captured man locked eyes in a silent struggle of wills. "Why are you staring at him, Merrick?" Maxson sharply said, breaking the silence because he could take no more of the tension. Put queries to him that you need answered! Why do you wait for this?"

Merrick did not waver, his eyes unblinking. With a small tremble in his palms, Maxson aimed a revolver at the man and asked, "Who is your boss? How did you feel about Rufus?"

With an unwavering smile, the man responded to Maxson's warning, "It's obvious that this is your first time handling a pistol. Calm down, young one." He scoffed, brushing aside Maxson's attempt at coercion.

Ever the watchful one, Merrick examined the man's facial expressions and body language. He came to the conclusion that he would withhold information from them, even if they tortured him. The man was monitoring them calmly, evaluating their advantages and disadvantages with each step.

"I know from watching the CCTV footage of the incident at the parking lot and my car number that your men will be here soon," Merrick said, turning to face the man who had been apprehended. Respond to my inquiry.

I don't know why, but my father informed me that you are the hint I need to finish my task."

A sly smile returned from the man: "Maybe your father should have told you why if he was so clever." He laughed heartily.

A veiled girl was revealing the man's illicit dealings and killings on TV, with solid proof to back up her accusations. As they watched the broadcast, the audience gasped and muttered in shock.

The girl's demand to take the man's illicit assets and give them to the underprivileged and destitute closed the film.

On watching this Recordings on TV, gathered in an opulent hotel room, one of the guys stated to the other three, "I don't know what's happening." "We ought to exercise caution. Why is this girl acting in this way, and who is she? Most importantly, who killed Rufus? He was a powerful and well-known businessman who maintained a low profile. We lost our jewel. He was one of us, and he obeyed our commands without error."

An additional man inquired, "Now what should we do? Are there any other plans?"

"I have sent Pascal to gather all the information we need," a third man said, interrupting. He'll return with some knowledge and hints."

Whoa, said another man, "why him?"

"He has excellent detective skills and presence of mind," the third man retorted. Other than our four selves, no one knows him, and he is not famous. For the moment, he is the best choice."

All four were in agreement.

99

Chapter-8

With a splintering boom, the door exploded, and two big bouncers surged into the room.

"Mr. Pascal, are you okay?" One of them questioned in a rough voice.

Pascal gave him a nod. Merrick, positioned in the middle of the room with his fists clinched, drew the bouncers' attention away from Pascal.

Merrick met the charging bouncers head-on, but he was prepared. He sidestepped their blows and returned fire, sending one of them sprawling after a hard blow to the jaw.

Maxson and Axel raced over to join Merrick, and the three of them engaged in back-and-forth combat with the bouncers. Punches were flying everywhere during the intense brawl.

Pascal stood by and observed, his heart thumping fiercely. He understood that if the bouncers prevailed, he would be in danger, even though he was too weak to fight.

Something caught Merrick's attention out of the corner of his eye. He sidestepped a blow and wheeled to retrieve a thick iron rod from the supply closet.

Merrick struck one of the bouncers in the forehead with a loud shout as he swung the rod at him. The bouncer fell backward, his face dripping with blood.

Seeing that he was overwhelmed and outmatched, the second bouncer paused. Turning, he fled with Pascal right at his heels.

Pascal exhaled a breath of calm. Although he was safe, he was aware that this was only the start. It would be the return of the bouncers, and they would be seeking retribution.

Dropping the rod, Merrick turned to face Axel and Maxson. He murmured, "We have to leave this place." "They'll be back soon."

Both Axel and Maxson gave a nod of approval. With Pascal trailing closely after, they snatched up their possessions and fled the house quickly.

Their hearts thumping in their chests, they rushed through the streets. Although they were unsure of their destination, they were aware that they couldn't stay still for very long.

Pascal considered what had transpired as they fled. He'd never seen a man like this look so irate. Plus, he had never witnessed Merrick fighting like that. He was a formidable opponent.

Pascal arrived at the motel, occupied by the four men. Pascal's failure to return their calls annoyed the four men, but he had to explain that he was abducted and unable to do so. Upon learning this, the men were stunned and proceeded to question him on a number of topics.

Who took you hostage?

Are you aware of who they were?

Have you noticed their faces?

Pascal retorted that he had no idea who had abducted him and had never even laid eyes on them. However, he gave the men his word that the kidnapper was more cunning and powerful than he was.

Pascal remarked, "I didn't even realize he had been following me." "He caught me with cunning. I was really irresponsible. I ought to have exercised more caution."

“The abductor asked me why his father had been looking for him. But I was unaware of the identity of the kidnapper's father, but the kidnapper had deduced, through whatever means” Pascal said. "Maybe he's searching for you."

The four men exchanged glances. To safeguard their operations and expansion, they murdered numerous dads and families.

One of the men stated, "We should find out what we have left to clear."

Subsequently, they began discussing the girl who had provided the recordings to the television station.

Another man remarked, "We need to find her and get rid of her." "She's a liability."

The four men talked about how they intended to exact revenge on the girl and the kidnapper. They had made up their minds to kill anyone who dared to threaten them.

Pascal listened silently to their intentions. Although he was afraid, he knew he had to spend time with the four men. He was in need of their protection as he tried to find a way out.

Although Merrick and Pascal approached the media at various times, the media maintained they were unaware of the origins or the sender of the recording. Pascal told himself he needed to track down the girl who had provided the tape.

Turning to face Maxson, Merrick stated, "We need to track down the girl who supplied those recordings. I don't understand. Why does she claim to have slain Rufus so much? Without the two of you, no one was around me. How was she able to kill Rufus? And why is she acting so dramatic? Rufus and she must be connected in some way. I need to locate her."

Pascal had prepared for and left a function after receiving an invitation. Upon arrival at the event, Pascal was warmly greeted with honor. Pascal arrived at the event to find his unlocked home devoid of any security personnel. He was living by himself.

Merrick intended to break into Pascal's house and take his laptop while he was at the event. Merrick wore goggles for night vision and was by himself. He looked around to make sure anyone was there, but it appeared to be empty. He leaped through the wall and entered the house. He went through the hallway and across the lawn, unlocked the door, and went inside.

Something within a room startled him. Although he felt that someone was in the house, he examined the room and found no one. After looking through Pascal's possessions for a few minutes, he discovered the laptop.

The noise in the room grew louder and closer to him. Someone gave Merrick a punch in the face when he turned around. Merrick's night vision goggles dropped to the ground as he sensed pain. He had trouble making out the shadow.

The shadow attempted to steal the laptop, but Merrick obstinately stood his ground. When he finally succeeded in turning on the lights, he was startled. He was perhaps one or two years older than the girl there. She appeared stunning and was fighting skillfully.

"I just need the laptop," inquired the female. Please don't let me harm you.

With a giggle, Merrick exclaimed, "What? See who injures whom."

For several minutes, Merrick and the girl fought. Merrick pushed the girl to the ground, wearing her out and weakening her. The girl cried, "Please, I need the laptop," as he tried to take the laptop and move on. I just must have this."

"Wait, are you the one who sent those recordings to TV, admitting that you killed Rufus and showcased his crimes?" Merrick inquired after pausing for a while.

"Yes," the girl answered. That animal ruined my life. However, he was only a pawn., some monarchs must be deposed. I really need this laptop." "He destroyed so many lives, including mine," Merrick remarked. So, follow me. We are able to collaborate." The young lady gave a nod.

Bailey, Merrick, and Maxson went back to Merrick's new home. Maxson questioned Merrick about why he hadn't introduced him to his girlfriend when they first entered, seeming astonished.

He shouldn't overthink things, as Merrick advised him. Bailey was Rufus's nemesis, and he had just recently met her. She had provided the recordings to the TV station. She was their ally from now on, and they would all be cooperating to facilitate the completion of their task.

Once their conversation was over, Merrick took Pascal's laptop out of its case and placed it on the table. Then she inquired of Merrick where they could obtain Pascal's fingerprint because they required it to unlock his laptop.

In response, Merrick said that he had taken Pascal's fingerprints during his abduction. Bailey laughed.

Maxson questioned Bailey about her claim of killing Rufus on the recording. With a laugh, Bailey explained that she had said what she had said because she had run out of options and didn't know what to do next. She'd said it without really thinking it through.

Merrick asked Bailey if she was crazy. He warned her, saying it could have resulted in her death. In addition, he inquired about her knowledge of Rufus's killer. Bailey inquired, but Merrick said it was him.

Bailey expressed her admiration and admitted that she had misjudged him. She assured him that he was capable of taking down the network. Merrick refuted this, claiming they were at a standstill at the moment. He advised them to identify their target, devise a strategy, and then choose when to take action. Bailey concurred.

Shocked, Axel opened the laptop and showed Bailey what was inside. Merrick and Bailey exchanged a glance of recognition.

Okay, Axel said, "It's open." "What do you want me to do?"

Merrick instructed, "Start going through the files." "See if you can find anything that can help us."

Axel quickly discovered something startling once he began browsing through the data.

Axel said, "Guys, you need to see this."

Bailey and Merrick rushed to Axel. Their eyes grew wide with surprise as they all turned to gaze at the TV.

"What the hell is this?" Bailey enquired.

"I'm not sure," Merrick replied. "But it's clear that Pascal was involved in some shady things."

As Axel went through the files, they discovered more and more proof of Pascal's participation in the network.

This, Maxson remarked, "is huge." "This could be the break we need."

Merrick gave a nod. It's enormous, he declared. "But we must exercise caution.

As they went over the files, the four of them talked about their findings and made plans for the future. They were aware that it would be risky and challenging.

"Now I see why my father told me that finding Pascal would give me an idea of what was happening and how to lead," Merrick remarked after taking a long breath. Up until now, Pascal was the one impeding our progress. Now that's evident. We may proceed without hesitation and make the necessary plans."

When Pascal returned from the function, someone had taken his laptop and broken his lock. He quickly called one of the four men and informed them of the situation.

The man was enraged. He said, "How careless can you be?" "He stole your laptop while you weren't home, following you the entire way. You foolish idiot! Was there anything crucial on the laptop that would cause us problems?

"Almost everything, that's right," Pascal apologized. "All of the complaints, frauds, and unauthorized and illegal documents are available there. We're going to get busted if he opens that laptop."

With disgust, the man on the phone spat. The man on the phone expressed his disgust and said, "A young man who's probably half of your age has humiliated you. I should never have trusted you."

Pascal admitted, "I know I made a mistake." "But I'll track down the boy, murder him, and retrieve the laptop. "How I do it doesn't matter."

"I anticipate that," the man uttered. "You are aware of our abilities. We are the fort's four walls of defense. Being the one who makes contact with the walls, you are the front guard. The unseen guard was Rufus. The young man removed Rufus. You got lucky, but he could have taken you out too. If he manages to go past the four of us, the strong one we work for will be the only one left. Even in the event that he murders everyone present, I am not convinced he can defeat him. I won't, however, take any chances. Before he discovers who, we are, we must destroy him."

"The laptop doesn't have any photos of you, but he might be able to find out your name," Pascal stated. "We ought to delay the opening of our new restaurant, in my opinion as well. We offered a complimentary first dinner to the first 500 customers. He'll be aware of this because he has my laptop and can access the calendar. He'll most likely be among the first 500 clients in the hopes of seeing the four of you."

The man talked to the other three males about this. "Let's not wait to open," he declared. "Now is the ideal time to get rid of him. He will ensure his own demise." He laughed slyly.

Back at his residence, Merrick laughed shrewdly too. He turned to face the other three men and added, "We should have a special lunch at the restaurant."

Chapter-9

Bailey, Axel, Maxson, and Merrick got together to plan their next course of action. "We need to be among the first 500 customers so we can get a look at the four men," added Merrick. "This is our chance to identify them and figure out how to take them down."

With a worried tone, Axel broke the silence. However, what about our security? They will definitely kill us if they see us. We ought not to endanger ourselves."

Merrick laughed despite Axel's concerns. Pascal will undoubtedly be present, and I have no doubt that he will quickly identify us and let them know. This is the only opportunity we have to be near them. We must no longer allow them to continue operating in secrecy."

Maxson chimed in, "But we can't just walk in there and confront them." "We need a plan."

Merrick gave a nod of approval. "I have a thought. Bailey will pretend to be unfamiliar with us and act like a stranger. Though Pascal will have seen all three of us, he will not know her. Bailey is going to be our

Secret agent; he'll monitor the four U r men and alert us to any movements."

Bailey appeared uncertain. I'm not sure, Merrick. This strategy seems hazardous.

Merrick gave her comfort. "Believe in me, Bailey. This is our best opportunity. Fear cannot prevent us from carrying out our necessary tasks."

They discussed it some more and came up with a final plan. Bailey would pretend to be a client and arrive at the restaurant first. Soon later, Merrick, Axel, and Maxson would arrive, disappearing into the throng. They would observe their surroundings while seated at various tables.

Merrick turned to his squad, and they got ready to leave. "Remember that we're in this together," he stated, his voice full of resolve. We'll stand with one another and eliminate those four men for good."

With their hearts racing with a mix of excitement and terror, they headed toward the restaurant. Even though they were aware that this was a risky undertaking, they were committed to making it work.

The eatery had an electrifying vibe. Individuals were hurrying and shoving one another in an attempt to obtain the coveted coupons that would entitle them to a complimentary lunch. Among the commotion, Axel's quick reflexes and deft moves allowed him to grab four coupons.

The management of the restaurant had set a 500customer maximum, and once that was met, no further patrons could enter. Pretending to be a regular customer, Bailey located Merrick, Axel, and Maxson seated at the adjacent table.

Merrick maintained a close eye on his surroundings, peering into the faces of other customers and searching for any indications of the four men as the minutes passed and the first orders began to come in. He encountered disappointment, though. There was no sign of Pascal, the man he was most anxious to locate.

Merrick was gnawing with frustration. He had thought that this would be the ideal chance to surprise the four men, but they had not materialized. If they didn't even show up at their own restaurant opening, how was he going to find them?

As the customers finished their meals and used their expiring coupons, the restaurant started to empty after a few hours. By seven o'clock at night, Merrick, Maxson, Axel, and Bailey-who was still going undercover as a stranger-were the only four people left.

Merrick slumped back in his chair, dejected. He was still nowhere nearer to discovering the four men, and their objective had failed. He couldn't help but question if his assessment of their slyness and capacity for hiding was off.

Five men were standing behind Merrick when he turned around and saw them. Pascal was standing among them, his face plastered with a smug smile. With their hearts racing in their chests, Maxson and Axel froze in fear.

One of the males spotted Bailey as she sat at the adjacent table. "Hi there, you! He growled, "Get out of here and go somewhere else to sit.

Bailey raised her head, startled and astonished. She questioned, her voice faltering, "Why?" "What's the problem?"

Another man took out a gun, his eyes icy and his face stiffened. Bailey turned and fled the restaurant without turning around as her eyes grew wide with fear.

With a sly smirk on his lips, the gunman turned back to face Merrick. "Been a long wait, hasn't it?" He made fun of it.

Merrick held his composure in the face of tension. "Well, it was worth it," he answered calmly.

The man laughed ominously. "Well, that concludes the game," he remarked. "It's time for this little mouse to meet his end."

With a steady expression, Merrick nodded. He remarked, "I knew this day would come."

Another man snarled, "We don't have time for your theatrics." "It's time to say goodbye."

With his rifle up, he aimed it directly at Merrick's chest. But Merrick showed no fear. Rather, he turned to face Pascal, who was observing the gathering silently, and said, "Please check your phone, Pascal."

Pascal paused, his gaze flitting from Merrick to the men with guns. Then, though, he took his phone out of his pocket. He opened it and started reading his texts.

The man with the gun lowered his weapon as Pascal's eyes widened in shock. His face took on a confused expression. He insisted, "What's going on?"

When Pascal's phone rang, he hurriedly took it out, and the photograph that had just been sent to him caused his eyes to widen in disbelief. It was a picture of Merrick, Axel, Maxson, and the four guys seated around a table. A covert camera within the eatery captured the image, making it evident.

Pascal was shouting "cunning girl" who had taken his laptop and leaked the recording of Rufus's confession, and he was aware that she was responsible for this. They were pawns in her own game, and she had been playing them all along.

Pascal felt rage flow through his veins. "It was her all along!" he exclaimed, sending echoes through the deserted eatery. "That girl, she's the one who's been playing us for fools!"

His eyes blazed with rage as he turned to face the four men. "She's the one who sent the recording to the TV station, the one who stole my laptop, and now she's the one who's trying to get us all killed!"

With a mixture of horror and incredulity on their faces, the four men exchanged glances. They had put their trust in Pascal, supposing him to be an ally and friend. But now they understood that he had been only a piece in Bailey's manipulative.

"We have to find her!" Pascal let out a shout. "We have to find her and kill her before she can send out that picture!"

With a nod of agreement, the four men's determination hardened. Bailey could not get away with this, not with them. They were going to track her out and get their revenge.

A feeling of worry descended upon Pascal as the fury left him. He was unable to disregard Merrick's caution. The four guys would be in great danger if they did not return safely.

Pascal leaned in to one of the four men and whispered something. With a nod of comprehension, the man turned back to face the others. He said, "We need to talk in private." "It's not safe here."

He gestured to a nearby parked automobile. Merrick and his buddies waited in the deserted parking lot as the four men climbed into the car and drove off.

Merrick looked at Axel, then at Maxson. Although they were all aware that they had to pursue the car, they also understood that doing so would be risky. Both numbers and weapons were against them.

Merrick groaned and got on his bike, leading the way with Axel and Maxson right behind. After several hours of driving through the countryside on twisting roads, they arrived at a vast, intimidating mansion.

When Merrick came up to the entrance, a security guard was in the way of his entry. A forceful "You can't go in here," declared the guard.

The driver of the vehicle, Pascal, pulled down his window and gave the guard a signal. After giving a nod, the guard moved aside, letting Merrick and his companions inside the mansion.

Valuable artwork hung on the walls, crystal chandeliers adorned the ceiling, and marble floors graced the lavishly furnished estate. They escorted Merrick, Axel, and Maxson into a spacious sitting room and ordered them to wait.

After a few hours, the three of them started to feel more nervous. They were clueless as to what was happening or how long they would have to wait.

At last, the sitting room door opened, allowing Pascal and the four guys to enter. As they sat down opposite Merrick, Axel, and Maxson, a nervous stillness descended upon the room.

After clearing his throat, Pascal started talking. With sadness in his voice, he replied, "I know you're all mad at me." "And with good reason. I duped all of you. However, I want you to know that I never intended to harm any of you.

A powerful and frightening voice emerged from one of the men, breaking the silence. He inquired, "What do you want, boys?" "What's the exchange for the stolen laptop?"

Merrick said nothing, keeping his eyes on Pascal. He had no desire to strike a deal and no purpose for haggling with these folks. Retaliation was the only reason he had come.

Sensing Merrick's determination, Pascal jumped right in. His voice filled with desperation: "We'll give you an amount of money you could never imagine"-the kind of money you'd need years to spend. Is that not sufficient communication?"

Merrick gave him a headshake. "I can make more money than you can ever give," he said in a tone that was icy and uninterested. "Money is not what I seek."

Merrick's lack of interest in riches intrigued one of the men, who raised an eyebrow. He screamed, "Then what is it that excites you?" "Everyone has a purpose or inspiration. Which is yours?"

Merrick gave a brief, sarcastic laugh. Merrick laughed briefly and sarcastically, remarking, "If that's true, then retaliation motivates me," his eyes gleaming with a sinister sheen.

The men looked at each other nervously, their laughter fading. They had misjudged Merrick, misjudging the intensity of his rage and the raging desire for vengeance that consumed him.

One of the men asked again, his voice full of doubt: "Revenge?" "Are you even aware of what you're requesting? We are dead if we expose who we were working. At least We will be hauled to prison and made to live behind bars for the remainder of our lives, even if you decide to keep the laptop."

He stopped to give his remarks time to register. Then he went on, a little softer in tone. "But we'll offer you something worthwhile in exchange if you return the laptop to us. A restaurant you can run with your buddies that is valued at crores of dollars A fresh start is significantly more advantageous than seeking retribution."

Leaning forward, he begged with his eyes. "Take your time," he commanded. "You have until tomorrow to decide. Till then, feel free to remain here. We're hoping you'll decide wisely."

The men exited the room with that, leaving Merrick, Axel, and Maxson alone. The prospect of a comfortable existence was pitted against a fierce need for retribution, weighing heavily on their choice.

Merrick, Axel, and Maxson woke up from their restless sleep as dawn broke, spilling a gentle light through the mansion's windows. They looked at each other warily, ready to face the men again. The tension from the night before was still hanging thick in the air.

With a determined expression on their faces, Pascal and the other four men went into Merrick's room. Pascal had become haughty instead of desperate, his eyes bright with a sense of authority.

"Have you made your decision, Merrick?" Pascal questioned, his tone brimming with conceit. "Are you ready to accept our offer?"

Maxson firmly shook his head. He stated, "We've told you before," in an unyielding voice. "Your assets and money are not what we seek. We're looking for a lead. We're curious as to who is in charge of you.

With his eyes narrowed and his mind racing, Merrick stayed silent. He felt there was a catch-a trap beneath Pascal's haughty exterior.

Pascal gave Maxson a nod while grinning mischievously. "Excellent," he remarked. "Then it's time to find that little rat."

His voice brimming with hatred, he turned to face Merrick. He said, "Check your phone." "It's your turn."

As Merrick reached for his phone and unlocked the screen, his fingers trembled, and his pulse raced. A rush of fear passed over Merrick as he viewed the image that had just been provided to him.

The image showed Bailey restrained and unable to speak, her eyes bulging with fear. The stolen laptop, a sobering reminder of the peril they were in, lay next to her.

Merrick glanced at Maxson and Axel, their expressions filled with shock and terror. In a raspy, desperate voice, he yelled, "Run!"

Maxson moved toward the window without thinking, looking out for a way out. He noticed some pipes running up the building's side; the metal of the pipes shone brightly in the early morning light. His muscles strained as he quickly grasped the pipes and started to climb, his whole weight dragging him downward.

As all of this was going on, Axel and Merrick ran, hearts racing, towards the door. Aware of the disturbance, Pascal gave his bouncers directions in a loud voice that reverberated throughout the mansion.

With intent evident, the hefty men who were the bouncers moved toward Merrick and Axel. The bouncers' expressions hardened. As soon as Merrick and Axel arrived at the edge of the compound wall, a massive barrier that appeared impassable, they realized they were stuck.

Merrick bowed, his back making a makeshift platform with a last-ditch effort. With his hands stretching for the top of the wall, Axel sprang onto Merrick's shoulders, sensing his friend's intentions.

Merrick staggered to his feet, feeling Axel's weight pressing down on him. Axel's grasp tightened on the wall, though, and he was determined. He gave a last heave and raised himself up, his body going through the barrier.

Tired and exposed, Merrick faced the approaching bouncers. They had their hands extended, prepared to grab hold of him. All that mattered was that he had managed to assist Axel in escaping.

Merrick cried out in agony as the bouncers closed in, his voice resonating throughout the enormous estate. He squinted, preparing himself for what was about to come.

Chapter-10

Axel bounced over the wall of the compound and hit the hard dirt outside with a thump. Heart thumping in his chest, he climbed to his feet and glanced around for Maxson.

But Maxson had vanished from view. When maxon realized that Merrick was still inside the estate and vulnerable to Pascal and his men, a feeling of terror swept over him.

Axel's thoughts we re racing, trying to decide what to do next. Maxson knew he couldn't abandon Merrick to his fate or return to the estate without being discovered.

Maxson let out a frustrated yell, torn between his dread for his own safety and his allegiance to his friend. Feeling impotent to save Merrick from their foes, he felt like a coward.

Maxson turned and walked toward his bike, which he had left parked nearby, with a heavy heart. He got on the bike and rode off, fearing that Merrick would take over his thoughts.

A car arrived at the residence just as Axel was leaving. The bouncers pulled a tied and gagged Merrick out, his face twisted with agony. Pascal stepped closer to him, hate burning in his eyes.

Pascal sneered and kicked Merrick in the chest, saying, "You're finished, Merrick." "You're just a dead fish now."

Despite the pain shooting through his body, Merrick laughed. His speech hoarse from the gag. "Physical pain doesn't affect me," he said. "You can't hurt me."

Pascal's shocked eyes grew wide. Never before had he seen anyone so fearless and unafraid of dying. A knot of uneasiness formed in his stomach, but he pushed it aside quickly.

"We'll see about that," Pascal scowled and gestured to the recently arriving automobile.

As the car approached the estate, Merrick's curiosity grew. He pondered the identity of this unexpected guest. He had no idea how drastically this experience would alter his life.

A man emerged from the vehicle; his features hidden by the darkness. Pascal was standing with his guys by Merrick's side when he walked up to him. The man handed Pascal Merrick's stolen laptop without saying anything.

Pascal's ideas were coming together, and his eyes were beaming with joy as he gripped the laptop. "Get these two kids into the room," he commanded his soldiers as he turned to face them. They must leave by tomorrow, making this their final day.

The bouncers seized Bailey and Merrick, leading them into a dimly lit room deep within the estate. Bailey's eyes were wide with panic as she tried to keep up with her hands cuffed tightly behind her back. Despite his injuries, Merrick did not back down, keeping his eyes on Pascal.

Merrick and Bailey shared a sympathetic glance as the room's door slammed shut, leaving them in complete darkness. Even though they were well aware of how dangerous they werc, thcy held on to hope.

Hours of quite ended when Bailey's voice shattered the suffocating silence. Her voice quivered as she said, "Merrick, I should have been more careful." "I never thought they would track me down, and now things have gotten out of hand. We must figure out how to get out of here."

With a tinge of sadness in his voice, Merrick laughed quietly. "I'm sorry for dragging you into this, Bailey," he replied. "You didn't deserve this."

Bailey shook her head, tears sparkling in her eyes. "Merrick, it's not your fault. We'll figure out a way out because we're in this together. We must.

Merrick gave a nod, his eyes lighting up with resolve. Merrick resolved that Pascal and his soldiers must not prevail. They needed to get away, not just for Axel and Maxson but also for themselves.

Bailey's voice dripped with despair, her sentences oozing resignation. With a scarcely audible murmur, she added, "It's all over, Merrick." "We're lost."

Anger flashed in Merrick's eyes. "Don't say that, Bailey!" he yelled, his voice resonating through the empty space. "We're not adrift. We're just getting lucky late."

Bailey furrowed his brows in perplexity. "What are you talking about, Merrick?" she questioned, a hint of doubt in her voice. "How can we hope to emerge victorious when we are completely at the mercy of these individuals, with our lives precariously balanced?"

A mixture of melancholy and resolve entered Merrick's eyes as his countenance softened. His voice was firm and quiet as he replied, "I know we're in danger, Bailey." Furthermore, I am aware that we might not survive this ordeal. However, I trust Maxson."

With a sneer, Bailey's laughter reverberated across the space. "Maxson?" she asked again, her tone showing her incredulity. "How about him? He's not fit to fight and would be better off avoiding these men than taking them one-on-one. He lacks the expertise and the leadership abilities to assume control. You are the one with all the knowledge about these individuals and the know-how to proceed. If you leave, what happens to our plan?

With unshakeable belief in his gaze, Merrick shook his head. "Maxson will find his way," he stated in a stern tone. "I have faith in him."

Bailey's doubt persisted because she was having trouble understanding Merrick's unshakable confidence in Maxson. "But why haven't they killed us yet?" she inquired in a curious tone of voice. "If they're planning to get rid of us, why haven't they done it already?" Merrick's gaze grew narrower as his brain began to piece the puzzle together. "There must be a reason they're keeping us alive," he stated. "They don't usually exhibit mercy.

Before they kill us, they must have some sort of plan for us, something they need us for."

Bailey's thoughts raced, attempting to comprehend the possible goals Pascal and his men might have for them. Why would they want to keep them alive anyway?

As the evening progressed, hunger continued to gnaw at Bailey and Merrick's bellies, and their bodies grew weary from neither eating nor sleeping. They made an effort to go to sleep, but the weight of their approaching doom was weighing down on them, consuming them with terror and uncertainty.

The minutes seemed to linger forever as the hours passed. Six figures emerged from the cracked door, their faces hidden by the gloomy light.

With her voice just audible, Bailey said to Merrick, "There are six of them."

Merrick's gaze raced around the room, examining the figures with a mixture of defiance and terror. He recognized four of the men; their faces burned into his mind from earlier interactions. However, the stranger with the shadowy face behind the others and towering stature behind them was the fifth figure.

Pascal moved forward and grinned cruelly at Merrick, his voice brimming with resentment. "Well, Merrick, this is the man you've been looking for," he mocked. The one we all serve. And now is the time when your dream of dying is fulfilled. Merrick, are you happy now?"

The unidentified man laughed softly, his tone gravelly and low. Whispering something into Pascal's ear, he leaned in close. Pascal nodded, his face becoming sterner.

Pascal pulled up his revolver and pointed it directly at Bailey. Bailey's mouth formed a wordless cry for pity as her eyes became wide with fear. However, Pascal had a callous heart and a heartless mentality.

A loud gunshot shattered Bailey's life, reverberating across the room. Her body went limp, and her eyes stared blankly into the distance as she dropped to the ground.

Merrick's heart fell like a stone as he stared in terror. He watched as tears filled his eyes and clouded his vision, taking the life out of Bailey's body. He let out a sob, a heartfelt cry of pain and hopelessness.

With Merrick alone with the stranger and just his suppressed sobbing breaking the silence, the five men turned and exited the room. Merrick experienced a sharp spike in his rage and a fierce thirst for retribution. Soon, an overpowering sense of hopelessness overtook him as he realized he was stuck and powerless to avoid his fate.

The man turned on the light, casting a harsh, merciless glare over the space. Silently, Merrick and the stranger fixed their gazes on one another, engaging in a wordless struggle of wills.

Merrick broke the silence, his voice shaking with anger. He yelled, his fists clenched in rage, "You coward!" "Release me! I will consign you to hell."

The stranger approached Merrick with unflinching calm and unblinking eyes. He freed Merrick's hands and threw him a water bottle without saying anything. With comfort in his dry throat, Merrick swallowed down the water.

Driven by fury and despair, Merrick sprang forward, slamming his fists into the stranger's face and abdomen. But the stranger was shockingly powerful and agile for his age. With ease, he parried Merrick's strikes, his movements accurate and quick.

Merrick was no match for the stranger's expertise and ability, even in spite of his youth and power. The stranger struck Merrick with blows that sounded like hammers, each one sending shockwaves of agony through his body.

Merrick felt his breath freeze in his chest as his neck tightened. He attempted to scream, but nothing came out. He was fighting to remain conscious as the agonizing pain caused his vision to become blurry.

The stranger delivered a last, crushing strike that was nearly imperceptible to the unaided eye, striking Merrick in the throat. A searing pain tore through Merrick's throat muscles and vocal cords.

His mouth filled with blood, and he began to cough uncontrollably. Merrick fell to the ground, staring up at the stranger's expressionless face with wide eyes filled with fear.

"It could be that your desire for retribution has led you to this point," the unfamiliar man remarked, sounding emotionless and icy. However, my past is worse than you could ever think. It has hardened and sculpted me. And it has strengthened me far more than you."

The stranger permanently silenced Merrick with a last, crushing blow. Merrick's life vanished abruptly, with his final breath trailing off in a quiet murmur. The stranger just stood there, staring at the corpse in front of him. A small smile crossed his lips, a terrifying reminder of his control over life and death.

Chapter-11

Humiliation and terror overwhelmed Maxson as he and Axel arrived back at their home. The sense that he ought to have done more to save his sibling persisted in his mind. He knew it wasn't his fault, but he still felt like a coward for it. He had turned around and fled, leaving his brother to deal with his destiny on his own.

Maxson cried out in agony, the guilt too great to bear. He repeatedly struck the wall, leaving his fists battered and bloody. Axel's attempts to stop him did not prevent Maxson from being immersed in his own misery.

"Why is this happening to me?" Maxson let out a cry. "Everyone in my family is dead. All I am is a coward. I have nothing to live for. What a dehumanizing, self-centered way to go."

It was impossible to handle the ache. In a fit of rage, Maxson ripped up the room and broke pieces of furniture. "I watched helplessly as my sister and brother were taken from me," he screamed, crying. I can no longer put up with this cowardice, and I was powerless to stop those who ruined my family. I int end to take my own life."

A file dropped from the top shelf as he crashed through thc cupboard. Maxson rctricvcd it. Documents in the file disclose a sinister secret that has the power to alter everything.

Maxson recognized Merrick's file as soon as he opened it. He stopped crying and opened the file, his eyes getting bigger as he saw his father's and brother's pictures. The package contained a few unidentified locations and photographs as well. He saw two letters at the end of the file. One letter appeared to be older than the other.

Maxson glanced at the new-looking letter first. The message read, "To Maxson from Merrick." When he had finished reading the letter to himself, tears welled up in his eyes. At last, he realized what his brother had intended.

The second letter was ancient, tattered, and covered in dust. He took it up then. Despite the difficulty of the letters, Maxson began to decipher them. "This letter is from father to son, Merrick," reads the title. Compared to the first letter Maxson had read, this one was somewhat longer and written in small type. Maxson's eyes welled with tears as he read the letter. After he had finished the letter, his mood started to shift.

Maxson's tears stopped, and his gaze remained unwaveringly strong. All he felt was a yearning for something very specific.

After closing the file, he returned it to the cabinet. After that, he got up and left the room. Axel sensed that his friend had undergone a transformation, even if he remained silent.

Maxson took a lofty stance and had a fierce look in his eyes. "I'm not a coward anymore," he told himself. "I used to be a nice and compassionate man, but going forward, I'll be a vicious, heartless, egotistical man. I'll do whatever it takes to reach my objectives. No more justifications or anxieties. I'll demonstrate my qualities to the world."

His voice was firm and authoritative as he called out for Axel. Axel stepped closer to him; worry written all over his face. "Maxson, are you certain you're, okay? You ought to get some sleep."

In response, Maxson said in a loud, frigid voice, "I don't need food, sleep, or anything that weakens me. Axel, I'm not the Maxson you believe me to be. I will fight until my last breath, and I'm willing to give everything up. I've changed as a man."

His strong and penetrating gaze remained fixed on Axel. "The last time you offered to assist me in saving my sister, Axel, once more, I beg for your assistance. Will you join me and help me on these dangerous adventures we have ahead of us? Good times and wonderful memories are coming to an end. just anguish, unrest, and grief. But I can assure you that if anything bad happens to you, I will be the one to defend you."

Axel acknowledged the seriousness of Maxson's plea with a sad nod. Despite knowing that his friend had undergone a significant metamorphosis, Axel was resolved to support him.

"It's time to conquer and create a new world!" exclaimed Maxson, filled with a wave of rage and resolve.

Maxson radiated confidence and fearlessness as he strolled down the busy street with Axel. He kept a close eye on everyone around him, noting their facial expressions and feelings. Maxson and Axel found a nice coffee shop after a mile and made the decision to stop for a rest. Maxson ordered a coffee from the waiter as they sat down at a table and started observing the people around him. He looked closely at their faces, attempting to read their emotions and thoughts from their subtle facial expressions.

Axel, in the meantime, mumbled, "Max, I'm afraid I don't have any money on me. Have you got enough money to pay the bill?

Maxson looked around the coffee shop and saw a man staring at his phone. He looked well-dressed and rich. Maxson walked up behind the man without thinking, carefully removing his wallet from his chair. He took out the money from the wallet fast, not even touching the cards, and slipped it back under the chair. Maxson went back to his table and sat quietly, keeping Axel's observant eyes off of him.

But Axel couldn't get rid of his uneasiness. He didn't like how impetuous and dishonest Maxson was acting. Unaware of his loss, the man whose wallet had been taken signaled the waiter as they waited for their bill. The man remained absorbed in his phone, completely oblivious to what was happening.

The man felt for his wallet when the server handed him the bill, only to find it gone. His eyes darted around the coffee shop as he hurriedly explored the area. When he eventually did find his wallet beneath his chair, He was shocked to find that the money was missing, but the cards remained intact.

Maxson watched the man closely, recording his motions, facial expressions, and body language as he responded to each situation. The man's range of emotions, from confusion to fascination, intrigued him.

Surprisingly, the man handled the incident with poise and composure. Seemingly uncaring about the lost money, he just swiped his card and carried on. He made no effort to track down the thief or even locate the pilfered money. Rather, he left the coffee shop fast, as if he were in a rush.

Maxson and Axel departed the coffee shop after a little while, but their thoughts were still focused on what had just happened. Maxson believed he could change the world one act of kindness at a time and experienced a sense of purpose and empowerment.

Maxson enjoyed the cool sea wind and the feel of the sand on his bare feet as he and Axel strolled down to the beach. He stared at the colorful group of people taking in the seaside scenery and the captivating sound of the waves lapping on the coast. Ever the cool-headed one, Axel trailed close behind, taking in Maxson's exuberant enthusiasm.

They strolled along the beach for a while before coming to a busy area where freshly caught seafood was being sold, including fried fish, prawns, and crabs. Attracted by the enticing smell, Maxson went up to the store and placed an order for Axel and himself for a dish of fried fish and prawns.

Maxson was thrilled with the food's flavor and quality as they sat down to enjoy it. He told the storekeeper how much he appreciated her tasty food. "Care for another plate, Axel?" he inquired, turning to face Axel.

Retaining his fullness from the last meal, Axel graciously declined, choosing instead to watch Maxson enjoy his feast. After they had completed their dinner and paid the bill, they greeted the shopkeeper, who invited them back and assured them that she would make even more delicious food.

Maxson and Axel carried on with their trek down the beach, their thoughts occupied with the sights, sounds, and tastes of being by the sea. Rejuvenated by the crisp air and filling dinner, Maxson found his motivation and resolve restored.

While walking on the beach, Maxson and Axel noticed a watch store a short distance away. Maxson, who has a thing for chic accessories, made the decision to look it over. As soon as he walked into the store, he saw a watch that drew his attention. He thought it would be a wonderful fit for his taste because it was sleek and modern.

He went up to the proprietor of the business and requested to view the watch. Maxson's curiosity caught the owner's attention, so he told a small child who worked there to get the watch from the display rack. The boy's palm brushed the rack as he reached for the watch, knocking several other timepieces to the floor with a clatter.

Furious at the child for his negligence, the store owner held up his hand and gave him a hard slap on the cheek. "Do you not have eyes? "Take care handling the merchandise!" he chastised.

The child winced, embarrassment and dread visible in his eyes. He begged the owner not to reduce his pay as he bowed his head and spoke tremblingly. I can't save anything, and it's already barely enough to cover my expenditures. You are free to strike or kick me to your heart's content, but please do not deduct my wages."

Maxson experienced a wave of rage and disgust at seeing this sight. "Why did you slap him?" he asked the store owner as he moved nearer. Rather than using physical force, you might take the cost of any damaged goods dircctly out of his paycheck."

Surprised by Maxson's help, the proprietor attempted to defend his conduct by saying, "He's just a reckless boy who doesn't pay attention." He must develop greater caution."

Maxson gave a disapproving shake of his head. Regardless of their transgressions, this manner of treatment should not be applied to anyone. There are more effective methods of training people."

"Can you please put this watch on my wrist?" Maxson requested, turning to face the boy.

The boy nodded cautiously and came up to Maxson, still shaking from the ordeal. Maxson purposefully slipped his hand while he was gently tightening the watch strap, letting the watch fall to the ground and break.

Maxson cast a determined glance at the owner of the store. It is obvious that this boy is not a good fit for your store. Come to an agreement."

Maxson examined the sight before him, and his eyes narrowed. The youngster was treated callously by the store owner, which inflamed his sense of justice and made him seek retaliation. He walked up to the owner with a hard resolve, his voice unflinching.

"I will give you the money you have earned today, your maximum daily profit, in exchange for the boy's job," Maxson proclaimed, staring directly into the avaricious eyes of the owner.

The owner, startled at first by Maxson's boldness, soon recovered his composure. The promise of a quick payment influenced his decision-making, leading him to accept Maxson's offer without hesitation.

But the child begged for another chance from the owner, his heart heaving with despair and rage. He begged, "Please, sir, I beg you to reconsider," his voice quivering with anguish. "I swear to put in more effort and to exercise caution. Don't let me leave, please."

Despite the boy's earnest plea, the owner's heart remained hardened due to his avarice. He yelled, "You're no longer of use to me," as his voice reverberated throughout the store. "Find another job!"

Maxson stepped in again, unwilling to stand by and watch such injustice continue. He put a pile of cash on the counter and said, "This is the money you demanded." "The boy will oversee the shop for the rest of the day in accordance with our arrangement. He will supervise you as you work, and you will give him your entire day's pay at the end."

The store owner, taken aback by Maxson's sudden kindness for a minute, rapidly estimated the possible earnings. He understood that the money Maxson had provided greatly outweighed his daily earnings, even in the unlikely event that the boy made extraordinary sales. Grinning slyly, he accepted the conditions.

Maxson and Axel turned to walk away, leaving the child alone with his confused feelings. Feeling vindicated, he observed as the owner unwillingly started to follow his orders.

Maxson's gesture of generosity made the youngster aware of the genuine essence of humanity, even in the midst of the day's tumult. He realized that not everyone was driven by avarice and self-interest, and that compassion and justice still mattered to some people.

The child went about his tasks with a renewed sense of commitment, spurred on by Maxson's unshakable faith in his abilities. He reorganized the shelves with great care, polished the timepieces with care, and greeted every customer with a real grin and excitement.

The boy's efforts paid off as the day went on. His upbeat demeanor and careful service drew customers, and sales grew over time. The store's earnings by the end of the day were far beyond the owner's most optimistic predictions.

When it came time to settle accounts, the owner, temporarily forgetting his greed, was overcome with shock. With wide eyes of surprise, he gave the youngster his earnings for the day.

The child thanked Maxson for the chance that changed his life, his heart overflowing with thanks. Not only had he kept his work, but he had also come to believe in people again.

Knowing that their acts had benefited the world, Maxson and Axel couldn't help but smile as they left the store. They'd restored the owner's sense of justice, taught the youngster a vital lesson, and made him feel like a valuable person again.

Chapter-12

Axel: (voice trailing off with frustration) Maxson, what are you doing? Is there anything about your work that is worth mentioning? You ought to be figuring out how to grant your brother's last wish. I promised to support you during your travels, but all you're doing is aimlessly strolling the streets and performing acts of kindness, as though you were some sort of Che Guevara, Mother Teresa, or Robin Hood. Who believe you to be?

Maxson: (laughs) I'm not one of the famous people you listed, but if everything in this world were flawless, easy, honorable, and truthful, I believe none of them would have faced accountability for their actions. Although they were regular people at birth, the world had an impact on them. They had no choice but to become well-known for their excellent deeds. I'm not just aimlessly wandering around like a tourist-I'm actively searching for the perfect spot to rest and begin my mission. Axel, adjust your viewpoint and see how everything is interconnected. All you have to do is adjust your viewpoint. I can never forget a part of my recollection, above all. A memory burns like fire, forever lodged in my head. Thus, if my brother were still alive, I would be doing just as he would. Despite the seeming contradictions in my acts, they are significant and related.

Maxson turned to face Axel and said, "If it's okay with you, may we go to the movies? With Presley, we've only seen one film together, and that was a long time ago. Do you want to go?"

With a heavy breath, Axel looked away. He gave a brief nod of consent.

Maxson reserved a cab to go to the closest cinema. When they got to the cinema, they purchased tickets for an English-dubbed film that would be starting in five minutes. When the movie started, they took their seats and got comfortable.

There were advertisements playing on the screen as the cinema filled with people. Axel and the rest of the audience stood up as the national anthem began to play and the lights went down. But Maxson and another teenage kid seated near the back of the same row did not get up from their seats. They remained seated till the anthem was over.

A middle-aged woman, perhaps 35 to 40 years old, yelled at the child in the corner of the auditorium who had stayed seated for the song as soon as it started playing. She cried, "Don't you have any sense of patriotism for the country?" "Did your parents raise you in this manner? What did you learn in college and at school? Could you please take a few minutes to stand up in respect for our country? These days, teenagers are simply not engaged!

After the woman's outburst created a commotion in the auditorium, the movie, which had barely begun, was put on hold. The boy, who had been sitting down, bent his head, feeling a flood of shame rush over him. Maxson got up and interrupted the woman because he could not take any more of her tirade.

"Wise woman, may I ask you a question?" he asked. The woman gave a brief nod. "So, except for the boy who didn't stand up for the anthem, you all were feeling patriotic for the country, right?" remarked the man. The woman gave a yes response.

"So why do you feel the need to impose your patriotism on other people?" Maxson asked. Why do you think it's necessary to criticize and humiliate someone for not acting in accordance with your beliefs? That's the antithesis of patriotism, right? Respecting others' freedoms of expression and belief is fundamental to patriotism, is it not?

Anger heated the woman's cheeks, and she opened her mouth to respond, but Maxson persisted. It is not patriotic to defend the national anthem.

Maxson's comments lingered in the atmosphere, casting doubt on the woman's sense of national pride. He went on to discuss the fundamental problem of corruption that afflicted their nation.

Maxson appreciated your patriotism and honor for the country, stating in a stern yet polite tone. "But I have to wonder, why weren't you able to demonstrate the same sense of patriotism by taking on the widespread corruption in our government? Why did you not raise your voice in opposition to the bribery, fraud, and hidden assets that deplete our country's resources? True patriotism is defending our nation's integrity, even in the face of hardship or public disapproval, rather than merely applauding the national song."

The woman felt the questions from Maxson searing her conscience as they resonated across the theater. He made her face the hard reality of their nation and put an end to her complacency.

His urgent question, "What about your contribution to reducing violence?" came out of his voice. Every day, you passively stand by while innocent lives are lost. If you saw a murderer pursuing an innocent victim, would you even have the courage to stop them?"

Maxson went on, his eyes unblinking. "And what about education, the essential component of any country's development? Why were you unable to demand that all children, regardless of their circumstances, have access to high-quality learning opportunities? Why were you unable to speak out against the gloom of illiteracy that so many of your fellow citizens are engulfed in?"

Not only was education a privilege, but it was also a fundamental right that would allow one to overcome ignorance and poverty. Why did you not see how urgent this problem was and how her silence had helped to keep inequity alive?

"And what about the plight of our children?" Maxson's voice was shaky with feeling. "Why did you ignore the exploitation of children's innocence, child labor, and child trafficking? Why don't you stand up for their defense and their entitlement to a secure and happy childhood?"

Why don't you imagine a small child who was troubled by the thought of having to work long hours in unfavorable conditions? Why didn't you take into account the difficulties faced by her society's most disadvantaged citizens?

Maxson's inquiries kept coming, each one serving as a sobering reminder of the difficulties his nation was facing. He discussed the devastation caused by overpopulation and deforestation, the frightening rise in unemployment, the hardships of the impoverished, the lack of infrastructure and connectivity in rural regions, and the growing drug addiction among young people.

The woman's sense of embarrassment grew with every query. Why did you let yourself get complacent and cozy in your own little world while your fellow citizens battled these urgent problems? Why have you not carried out your duties as a human being, a sister, and a citizen?

What made you allow deforestation to occur? Why did you not inquire about the depletion of natural resources? "What will you leave behind for future generations?"

Maxson's statements made her aware of a terrible reality. Being a patriot meant doing more than just flying a flag and playing the national anthem; it meant acting, improving the lives of others, and striving for a brighter future for everybody.

The entire audience was in disbelief when Maxson concluded his speech. He went on to say that he was disappointed in the audience's perception of patriotism. I'd like it if someone here tried to comprehend what true patriotism is all about. You only seem to be able to assault the poor, the disabled, and those without weapons. You don't have the guts to face those who shield themselves with wealth and power. You don't think being a patriot means more than supporting your nation during a cricket match or remembering Republic Day and the birthdays of leaders and liberation fighters. However, you are blind to the reality that exists all around you. You think that being a patriot just means welcoming people and applauding the national anthem. You want to be nothing more than photocopies, but you are like fresh pages out of a book. There are times when you unintentionally belittle your own patriotism in conversations. You have less regard for your own nation and more regard for people who have finished their education overseas. You gossip about the features of other countries that are similar to and different from your own. You still find reasons to be dissatisfied even though your country has given you freedom, food, housing, security, and privacy." Maxson finished his remarks and walked out of the theater. The theater made the decision to postpone the upcoming screening as the following show drew near.

Chapter-13

A lively crowd was milling about a few meters away from Axel and Maxson as they emerged from the theater. Intrigued, Maxson went up to a man nearby and asked him what was uproarious. The stranger answered in a slightly patronizing manner, "Haven't you heard? They are holding a lavish celebration in Mr. Walt's honor. We have even been blessed with the presence of the mayor himself."

Still confused, Maxson inquired, "Who is Mr. Walt? Why is everyone excited to welcome him so much? How did he come to be so well - known?"

Maxson's innocence amused the visitor, who laughed and remarked, "You seem to have a lot of questions, young fellow. This role is particularly crucial for youngsters such as yourself. Would you not be interested in learning ng more about this amazing person?

Inspired by the stranger's remarks, Maxson persuaded Axel to go to the event with him. A festive atmosphere permeated the function area as lights burst and music played, with dancers swaying to the beat.

Games and cultural acts kept the audience happy as the event got underway. There were just two sessions left as the evening came to an end: the mayor's speech and Mr. Walt's highly anticipated speech.

Grinning broadly, the mayor led Mr. Walt up to the platform, where he began his statement. "I am honored to have Mr. Walt among us today," he said. "Today, we gather here to honor Mr. Walt and present him with the prestigious 'Socio-Kind' award, recognizing his unwavering commitment to our society."

"You may all know Mr. Walt for his boundless love for our community, his unwavering support for education, and his deep compassion for the elderly," he said after pausing to give his comments some time to sink in. He has philanthropically contributed hundreds of crores to help those afflicted during natural disasters. He has committed his life to helping impoverished children have access to school and learning opportunities. He manages over ten trusts dedicated to assisting the underprivileged. To top it all off, he has generously offered to pay for studies in science. He is here today, prepared to open a brand-new senior living facility for our citizens."

"Mr. Walt is a true embodiment of simplicity and greatness," the mayor said in a voice resonant with affection as he ended. It is an honor for me to welcome him to the stage as we come to an end to this historic day."

A modest man with an air of wisdom, Mr. Walt approached the podium as the audience burst into cheers. Unlike the mayor's pompous speech, his was a speech free of self-aggrandizement. Rather, he discussed the value of empathy, community, and the effectiveness of group efforts.

He told tales of his efforts to encourage people to follow in his footsteps rather than to get attention or fame. He exhorted everyone in attendance-young people in particular-to realize their potential and have a constructive influence on thc world.

The audience was moved by Mr. Walt's Greatness and sincerity, and they erupted in deafening ovations as he finished his address. Axel and Maxson looked at one another with awe and respect for this man they had just met, a man who had completely changed their perception of what it meant to be truly great, shining in their eyes.

The audience erupted in resounding applause as Mr. Walt got up from his seat, their voices echoing throughout the large hall. With a modest smile, Mr. Walt got started, his voice brimming with conviction and honesty.

"I stand before you today, not seeking accolades or praise," he said. I am motivated by a strong sense of purpose and a desire to have a positive impact on the world. Giving assistance to people in need, relieving their problems, and making them happy brings me great delight."

He took a moment to process what he had said, looking from hopeful face to expectant face in the audience. "My ultimate goal is to lead by example and encourage people to adopt a selfless and compassionate attitude. I think that everyone has the capacity to have a good influence and to leave a legacy of charity and love."

He proceeded in a tone of mild encouragement, turning to the children seated in front of him. "Teens and young adults, break free from the chains of daydreaming and seize the chances presented to you. You have limited time, so make the most of this valuable resource. Instead of wasting it on meaningless fancies, direct your youthful energy toward worthwhile endeavors."

He delivered his emphasis on the strength of youth with conviction in his voice. "Remember," he said, "people frequently say that money is not as important as time and that character is more essential than health. But your greatest weapon, in my opinion, is your age. It is a vitality reserve that flows through your veins, protecting you from hardship. If you make good use of these gifts, you can open doors to success and attain prosperity, well-being, and a meaningful existence."

The gathering erupted in spontaneous applause as he wrapped up his address, moved by his knowledge and persistent devotion to changing the world. Mr. Walt gave them one last wave of thanks before leaving the podium. His words would live on in their memories, inspiring them to strive for a better future.

Maxson observed from a distance as Mr. Walt got into his car and drove off as the conference came to an end. He saw Pascal and the four men who had killed Merrick among the crowd leaving the event, and a wave of shock and rage ran through him.

His head was full of inquiries. What on earth were these merciless bandits doing at an event that the honorable and kind Mr. Walt was hosting? What made them follow

Walt's vehicle? A raging thirst for retribution consumed Maxson, and he realized he had to move fast.

He saw a man without hesitation getting ready to get off his motorcycle. Maxson lunged forward, forcing Axel to follow, and knocked the rider off his bike. The man lost control of his motorcycle and skidded to the ground.

Maxson and Axel hastily climbed atop the downed motorcycle and accelerated rapidly, chasing after Pascal's vehicle. Despite the heavy traffic on the streets, Maxson skillfully maneuvered around it, his reckless driving motivated by his determination.

They saw Pascal's car after driving for a few kilometers, and Walt's car was not far behind. Maxson trailed behind, his gaze fixated on his quarry.

Both automobiles drove on the same straight road for several minutes. But just as they were about to cross a street, Pascal's vehicle suddenly turned to the left and vanished down a side street.

Maxson was surprised at this abrupt shift in course. Pascal left Walt's car behind, but why? Was there another motive behind him, or was he just going to ambush Walt?

Though shaken, Maxson persuaded himself that he had to have misinterpreted the circumstances. His major concern was still getting revenge for his brother's death, and he believed that this was his only opportunity to do it.

Maxson kept going, following the route Pascal's Car had taken, his resolve restored. Whatever the reality was, he was ready to face it.

When the vehicle arrived at the Royal Hotel, Pascal and the other four men got out and vanished via the main door of the establishment. Maxson's heart raced with eagerness. He was certain that Pascal and his men were lodging in the hotel, and he realized he needed to figure out a way to join them.

However, their money was running low, so it was getting harder for them to buy a stay at the opulent hotel. Maxson was worried, but Axel calmed him, saying, "We'll work it out, Max. In the same manner as usual."

They stepped out onto the busy streets and passed businesses selling vegetables, clothes, and furniture, but none of these places looked like good places to stay. Their quest brought them to a glistening jewelry store with windows full of chains and priceless stones.

Maxson's gaze flitted here and there, planning a move. He stepped up to the counter and pretended to be interested in buying a chain. Unbeknownst to him, the thieving shopkeeper opened a box and showed off a collection of beautiful necklaces.

Axel and Maxson exchanged a sly look, and then they grabbed the whole box of chains and ran out of the store. The alarm went off, startling the staff, who took up arms.

With adrenaline pumping through them, Maxson and Axel swerved through the throng. A security guard grabbed Axel by the arm as they got closer to the exit. Without thinking, Maxson gave the guard a shove that knocked him to the ground.

Their hands jingling from the stolen chains, they dashed out of the jewelry store together. Although they had narrowly escaped apprehension, the threat persisted. Maxson knew hc had to face Pascal and his men shortly because they were still on the loose.

For Maxson and Axel to be able to afford to remain at the Royal Hotel, they realized they had to sell the diamonds as soon as possible. In an attempt to pawn the stolen chains, they approached the proprietor of a tiny jewelry pledging business after spotting it.

The astute businessman who owned the shop realized right away that the gems were stolen property. Though he might have easily called the police, he made a deal instead. Although he would pay a reasonable sum for the gems, it would be much less than their true value.

With no other option, Maxson and Axel grudgingly accepted the conditions set by the store owner. Although the value of the gems far exceeded the tiny sum of money they were given, it was still sufficient to book a room at the Royal Hotel.

When they checked in, they asked to be put in a ground level room. They requested a room, and the receptionist, not knowing what they were doing, gave it to them. Now that they were in their hotel room, Maxson and Axel started planning their next course of action. They needed a plan, but they also knew they had to face Pascal and his soldiers.

Maxson and Axel went to their hotel room in hopes of getting a little break from their never-ending chase. Maxson took a seat by the window and looked out at the busy hotel entrance, watching customers come and go. Their room had a direct view of the hotel lobby and was conveniently next to the exit.

He watched intently for the following few hours, getting more and more excited as the minutes passed. At last, well after midnight, Pascal and his four cronies left the hotel. A mixture of anxiety and excitement beat in Maxson's heart.

Though he was tempted to follow them right away, Maxson decided it would be wiser to wait until they got back to their rooms. They may then use this information to locate themselves precisely and launch a surprise attack.

Maxson stayed riveted to the window, his eyes relentlessly searching for Pascal's group, as Axel fell asleep. The night dragged on, Maxson's irritation growing with every hour that went by. Questions and doubts started to nudge their way into his consciousness. And if they hadn't made it back to the hotel, what if they'd abandoned their plans and gone somewhere else to hide?

Reluctant to give up, Maxson decided to keep up his watch, depriving himself of food and rest. He looked into the darkness, waiting for the telltale indications that would indicate Pascal's return, and his persistence kept him going.

At last, when midnight drew near again, a ray of hope flickered through the darkness. After a while, Pascal and his men reappeared, whispering conspiratorially. Maxson followed them carefully as they went to the first level and into the middle room.

Maxson left his room as quietly as a ghost, his actions driven by a rush of adrenaline. He followed Pascal's party carefully, staying well out of sight as they went up the steps.

When he got to the first floor, he saw them vanish inside the center room, their voices vanishing into the darkness. Maxson had located his objective.

Maxson quickly made his way back to his room and woke Axel up from his sleep. "Axel, get awake! It's finally time. "We have to take action right away!" he exclaimed; his voice full of resolve.

Startled by this abrupt interruption, Axel woke up groggy and ended up dripping water all over himself. Unfazed, Maxson gave Axel a knife while holding onto another.

With hesitation in his voice, Axel questioned Maxson's plan, his eyes still clouded over from sleep. "Maxson, do you think two of us can overpower five of them?"

With confidence in his voice, Maxson comforted Axel. Indeed, Axel. They're all old men, long past their prime, and we have Knives. To make them reveal their commander, we can threaten them."

Axel continued to feel uneasy. "What if they have guns?"

Maxson answered, taking a large breath out, "I don't think they do. When we last saw them, they were unarmed. If they have guns, we'll back off and wait for another chance. But we have to take this chance for now. It's our only opportunity.

Armed with their blades, Maxson and Axel moved resolutely toward the first floor's central chamber. Their hearts thumping together, they banged hard on the door.

❞

Chapter-14

Pascal stepped closer to the door, his heart thumping in his chest, as the menacing knocking reverberated around the room. His fingers shaking, he turned the knob, and the door creaked open, revealing Maxson and Axel standing in the entryway, their eyes glinting with menace and their faces hardened. Pascal felt his spine tingle as they clenched their blades, projecting a sense of menace.

Pascal tried to slam the door shut instinctively, but Maxson's foot shot forward, stopping Pascal's attempt. Maxson looked around the room, his eyes burning with an intensity that could cut through the thickest of walls. Five guys stood, unarmed, as he had expected, their faces etched with panic at realizing what a dangerous situation they were in.

Maxson felt a wave of vindictive rage flow through his veins. It was time for Maxson to seek vengeance for the abuse he had endured. Sensing chaos was about to break out, Pascal lunged toward Axel, trying to step in. However, his attempts were in vain since Maxson cut Pascal's stomach with his knife during an uncontrollably furious outburst.

A searing pain exploded from Pascal's abdomen, and his eyes dilated with shock. A pool of blood formed, turning his clothes scarlet. His breath came in shallow, desperation-filled gasps as he struggled to breathe. His vitality evaporated in a matter of minutes, leaving only a limp, silent body hunched on the ground. Maxson placed a letter in pascal's pocket to find who leads them.

The other four men screamed for assistance; their faces twisted with fear. However, the door was closed, so their shouts were muffled, and they were confined inside the chamber. With intense anger in his eyes, Maxson pursued the men, making his loud footsteps reverberate throughout the room as the scared men hurried to get away.

Maxson lunged toward the men, his head pounding and his lungs burning, his knife flashing like a lethal serpent. They collapsed one by one, their bodies giving in to his unrelenting pursuit. The atmosphere in the room turned gloomy as the smell of fear and blood permeated the space.

A sharp pain shot through Maxson's skull as he prepared to take out the last man. A night lamp struck his skull, throwing him back and causing him to stagger. His blood dribbled down his cheeks, distorting his vision.

When Axel saw his friend struggling, he roared with primordial anger. He made a quick, lethal motion and stabbed the last man in the heart, taking his life in an instant.

Axel collapsed next to Maxson, exhausted and bleeding; their corpses sprawled in the chaos they had caused. With the exception of the steady drip-drip of blood smearing the floor, the room became silent.

Lifeless bodies of the four men lay strewn across the floor, filling the room with the stench of death. With his face smeared with perspiration and blood, Axel attempted to wake Maxson from his unconscious state. "Maxson! Get up! He said, "It's not over yet," and shook Maxson's shoulders.

Maxson stammered unintelligibly, still dazed from the impact on his head. Understanding how serious the situation was, Axel lifted Maxson up onto his shoulders and stumbled out of the room.

Startled by their appearance, the hotel receptionist said, "What happened?" as they approached the desk. Why does he look like this?"

With a quick wit, Axel answered, "He fell in the bathroom after slipping. I need some assistance moving him to my bike because he is feeling lightheaded."

Without hesitation, the receptionist offered to help Axel pull Maxson onto the bike. Axel sat Maxson down so that he could rest his head on his shoulder and keep his balance.

Axel hurried to the closest hospital and gave the worried physicians the same rundown on Maxson's fall. The physicians quickly took Maxson to the intensive care unit as his health deteriorated.

Concerned for his friend's safety, Axel used the money they had left over from selling the gems to cover the needed advance deposit. He was waiting tensely for the doctor's report.

After a thorough inspection, the doctor returned and told Axel, "Maxson is stable now." All he needs is some sleep. He's now visible to you."

Axel hurried up to Maxson's bedside, feeling a wave of relief. "Axel, we should leave now," Maxson remarked as he began to regain consciousness.

They were watching the news broadcast while they waited for Maxson's discharge papers in the general waiting area. The newsreader declared that four men were found dead in the Royal Hotel under mysterious circumstances. The police have identified suspects in the case and are actively investigating. The police are confident that they will catch the offenders in the near future.

Maxson turned to Axel as he watched the television story and stated, "Axel, they might know where we are." It's best for you to go and avoid me until I get in touch with you. It is essential to our security."

Reluctant to abandon his friend in such a situation, Axel objected, saying, "No, Maxson, I won't leave you here."

"Axel, I can take care of myself," Maxson said. I'm able to eat, walk, and converse. Please be aware of how serious this situation is. I'll call you when I'm secure, and we can get back together."

Axel reluctantly accepted Maxson's proposal and departed the hospital.

The harsh voice behind him said, "Maxson, we have an arrest warrant for you," and Maxson's heart skipped a beat.

He turned around and saw two stern-looking police officers standing before him, their faces merciless and uncaring. The police officers showed Maxson the warrant, and he quickly glanced at it before nodding in agreement.

Handcuffed and escorted into the police jeep, Maxson was brought to the police station. A policeman approached Maxson as the investigation got underway, his voice snapping like a whip: "We know you and your friend killed those four men." We only need to know why you are acting the way you are and where your accomplice is. If you cooperate, you might be able to avoid this pain."

With a defiant expression on his face, Maxson said nothing and maintained his fixed stare. As the policeman's annoyance level increased, he gave the order for his colleagues to give Maxson a taste of their batons. Despite the constant beatings, Maxson remained steadfast and refused to give them the satisfaction of watching him break.

The policeman's tone became more aggressive as the questioning went on, saying things like, "Maxson, you're wasting your time." If you tell the truth, we might be willing to be lenient."

With a tone full of contempt, Maxson shot out, "Even if I poured my guts, it wouldn't change our predicament. It's a useless activity."

The policeman became enraged and gave the order for his men to beat Maxson harder in an attempt to break his spirit. Maxson fell into oblivion, his body smashed and damaged.

Maxson came to him after a few hours, a small stream of water bringing him out of his daze. With an air of urgency, a policeman announced, "You have a visitor." Come on over right away."

The policeman opened the cell door and motioned for Maxson to enter a dimly lit room. A lone figure stood in the shadows, waiting for him to approach.

Maxson's eyes narrowed as he looked up at the mysterious figure in the shadowy room. He demanded, his voice full of suspicion, "Who are you?"

The man moved forward, the one bulb in the room giving off a faint glow on his face. Maxson let out a gasp and widened his eyes in shock. Mr. walt?

Maxson felt a surge of anger run through him, his fists clenching tightly. He so badly wanted to lash out at this man, this embodiment of his misery and anguish. But he was aware that Walt, who was well-known for his ruthlessness and cunning, was unbeatable.

"Maxson, that's my name to the world," Walt said in a tone that was serene and almost comforting, as if he were unaware of Maxson's inner turmoil. Your father is no longer with us, but only he knew who I really was and what my goals were."

He paused, staring deep into Maxson's soul, saying, "Maxson, don't worry. My intention is not to murder you or imprison you. Actually, I've made plans for your release."

Maxson's perplexity increased. "Why?" he questioned, a hint of doubt in his voice.

"I will tell you later, but for now, just know that your time in this cell is over," Walt said with a mysterious smile.

Maxson was still confused, unable to make sense of Walt's behavior in light of his background. Walt was a depraved individual, a skilled manipulator who had planned his family's demise. And yet, here he stood, promising him liberty.

Maxson said to himself, "Walt is the most dangerous man I've ever encountered." "His appearances and actions are nothing more than a deceptive mask for the evil that lurks beneath."

He thought back to Walt's ruthless deeds: the icy killing of his sister, father, and brother; the annihilation of his entire family. Walt harbored a deep-seated animosity towards him, a vendetta that originated with Maxson's father.

Maxson was afraid, but he also saw the attraction of freedom. He was desperate to get out of his cell and exact revenge on those who had wronged him.

Maxson said, "Walt is powerful, even at his age." He is ruthless, clever, and crafty. Though his intentions remain unclear, one thing is clear: he should not be taken lightly."

Maxson kept thinking about Walt's final words, "We will meet again soon, Maxson."

A policeman came to Maxson's cell as dawn was breaking and motioned for him to follow. Maxson sneaked out of the police station under the cover of darkness, with excitement and trepidation mixed together in his heart. He was aware that Walt's Motto was a calculated move in a game of manipulation and retaliation rather than an act of kindness. Now that Maxson was a pawn in Walt's devious plan, facing the darkness that had taken over his life was the only way to get it back.

Chapter-15

Maxson found himself wandering aimlessly through the streets, his mind consumed by thoughts of Walt and the elusive enemy. He was miles away from the police station, with no clear plan of action. As he trudged along, a boy on a bicycle approached him and handed him an envelope.

Maxson's eyes widened as he recognized handwriting on the cover-it was Merrick's. With trembling hands, he opened the envelope and pulled out the letter inside. The letter addressed him, this is for you, not Pascal, filling him with a mix of anticipation and dread.

"My dearest Maxson," the letter began. "When you read these words, I will have already departed. I have spent the last seven years battling a formidable, powerful, and unknown enemy. Despite my best efforts, I have made little progress in getting close to him. Every time I risked my life in pursuit of revenge, I feared that if I perished, there would be no one to carry on the fight.

But then, I saw you. Our father had great faith in me, but I have failed him. You are our only hope and our last chance to bring this enemy to justice. I implore you, my brother, to not fail. And please read the letter from our father that is hidden beneath this one. It has been a source of strength and inspiration for me throughout my struggle. I believe it will do the same for you.

I wish you all the luck on your mission. May you succeed where I have failed."

As Maxson finished reading the letter, a wave of sadness washed over him. He carefully folded the paper and tucked it into his pocket. He picked up the discarded envelope and turned it over, his eyes widening in surprise as he noticed a street name and a time written on the back.

Maxson stood in the designated spot, his heart pounding in his chest as he awaited the next twist in this intricate game of deception and betrayal. The air was thick with tension, the silence punctuated only by the distant hum of the city.

When the envelope arrived, Maxson snatched it with trembling hands. As he tore it open, his eyes widened at the sight of the photographs enclosed within.

A chilling letter accompanied the photographs, its words dripping with menace and manipulation. It was from Walt, the elusive mastermind who had been orchestrating this macabre charade.

"Greetings, Maxson," the letter began, its tone laced with a sinister mockery. "I trust you received the letter from your brother. By now, you should realize that I am always watching, always one step ahead. I am the puppeteer pulling your strings, and you are merely a pawn in my twisted game."

Walt's words struck a chord of fear within Maxson. He had always known that Walt was powerful and dangerous, but the depths of his depravity were far beyond anything he had imagined.

"I demand an exchange for your escape from the cell," Walt continued, his voice echoing in Maxson's mind. "In exchange for your freedom, you must betray your friend, Axel. Lure him to me, and I will take care of the rest. I know you will do it, Maxson. You are weak and desperate, and I hold the strings that control your fate."

Maxson's blood ran cold as he absorbed the gravity of Walt's demand. The thought of betraying Axel, his loyal companion and confidant, filled him with disgust and despair. But he knew that Walt was not making an idle threat. He had the power and the ruthlessness to carry out his sinister plan.

"I and your father were good friends once," Walt continued, his tone shifting to a melancholic whisper. "But misunderstandings and betrayal drove us apart. I regret taking his life to this day. However, your father was not the innocent man you believed him to be. He committed countless crimes and murders under my orders, his hands stained with the blood of countless innocents."

Walt's words shook Maxson to his core. He had always idolized his father, a legendary figure shrouded in mystery. But now, Walt's revelations paint a chilling portrait of a man corrupted by power and greed.

"And then there was the hydrogen cyanide incident," Walt continued, his voice dripping with malice. "Do you recall the orphanage tragedy that claimed the lives of nearly four hundred children? That was my doing, carried out by your father, who was unaware of the orphanage's true purpose. He blindly followed my instructions, believing he was serving a noble cause."

Maxson's mind reeled as he absorbed this shocking revelation. The orphanage tragedy, a dark cloud that had hung over his childhood, was not merely a random act of violence. It was a calculated act of evil, orchestrated by Walt and unknowingly executed by his own father.

"I have attached photographs that serve as evidence of these crimes," Walt continued, his tone cold and detached. "If you refuse to betray Axel, I will be compelled to unleash another wave of terror. I will expose your father's crimes and connect them to the cyanide disaster, painting him as a monster responsible for the deaths of countless innocent children. You and Axel will be branded as his accomplices and fugitives from justice, and your entire family will be condemned by society."

Maxson felt a wave of despair wash over him. Walt's threats were not empty promises. He had the power and the ruthlessness to carry out his sinister plan. The lives of hundreds of children, the reputation of his family, and his own freedom all hung in the balance.

"The choice is yours, Maxson," Walt concluded, his words echoing in Maxson's mind. "Betray Axel and save yourself, or stand by your friend and face the consequences. Time is running out. Make your decision wisely."

Maxson stood there, clutching the envelope and the photographs, his mind consumed by a whirlwind of conflicting emotions. Maxson felt torn between loyalty to his friend and fear of Walt's retribution. The weight of the decision rested heavily on his shoulders.

Maxson's heart pounded like a drum as he wrestled with the agonizing decision that lay before him. Betraying Axel, his steadfast companion, felt like an act of treachery, a betrayal of the trust and camaraderie they had forged through their shared trials. But the thought of Walt's threats, the potential exposure of his father's crimes, and the imminent danger to innocent lives weighed heavily on his conscience.

After what seemed like an eternity, Maxson made his choice. With a heavy heart, he picked up his phone and dialed Axel's number. Axel's voice, filled with relief and excitement, greeted him on the other end.

"Maxson! Are you out? Where are you?" Axel inquired; his eagerness evident in his tone.

Maxson hesitated, his voice trembling as he revealed his location. Axel, without a moment's hesitation, sprinted towards the rendezvous point, his heart brimming with anticipation.

As Axel spotted Maxson, a surge of joy washed over him. He rushed towards his friend, embracing him tightly. "It's good to see you, Maxson," he exclaimed, his voice brimming with relief. "I knew you wouldn't let me down. Together, we'll overcome this."

Maxson, however, remained silent, his eyes filled with a mixture of guilt and regret. As Axel turned around, he froze in shock at the sight of armed police officers closing in on them. Confusion clouded his mind as he struggled to comprehend the scene unfolding before him.

The officers, their movements swift and precise, descended upon Axel, their hands reaching for him. "Come on, boy," one of them barked, his tone devoid of empathy. "Your time's up."

They forcefully pulled Axel towards their waiting jeep, ignoring Maxson, who stood frozen in place, his eyes filled with shame and remorse. Axel's heart sank as he watched Maxson's tear-filled gaze, the realization of his friend's betrayal dawning upon him.

Axel's heart weighed heavy as he was dragged away, his spirit crushed by the weight of betrayal. Maxson, alone and tormented, collapsed to his knees, his sobs echoing through the deserted streets. The crowd, drawn by the commotion, watched in silence, their whispers carrying the weight of judgment. Maxson, enveloped in his own despair, managed to stumble away from the scene, his heart shattered and his spirit broken.

Walt had announced that he would be holding an open donation drive for his orphanage in the bustling streets of the city. People greeted Walt with respect and admiration, eager to contribute to his noble cause. Walt and his assistants eagerly collected funds from the generous public, the crowd swelling with enthusiasm as they witnessed Walt's dedication to helping underprivileged children.

Maxson received news of the event and chose to confront Walt, demanding the commissions he had been promised for his work in collecting donations. He arrived at the scene, a donation box in hand, and began collecting funds from the crowd.

Walt, noticing Maxson's presence, felt a surge of confusion and apprehension. As Maxson approached him, he kneeled down and began shouting, "Sir, please give me my commission! You promised me 10% of the donations I collected, with 70% going to your personal gains and 20% to the orphanage. But you took all the money for yourself! This is unfair! Give me the commission I earned!"

Walt, taken aback by Maxson's outburst, tried to defend himself, denying any wrongdoing. "What are you talking about?" he retorted. "When did I say that? Who are you? Are you trying to damage my reputation?"

Maxson, undeterred, continued to expose Walt's deception. "Don't lie!" he shouted. "I've been working for you for the past two years, and you haven't even paid me my salary. You threatened me to death if I spoke out!"

The crowd, hearing Maxson's accusations, grew restless. Whispers turned into murmurs, and the flow of donations came to a halt. News channels, alerted to the unfolding drama, began broadcasting the scene live.

Walt, cornered and exposed, felt his frustration mounting. He tried to regain control of the situation, but Maxson's relentless accusations and the growing skepticism of the crowd were overwhelming.

The once-celebrated philanthropist was now facing the harsh reality of his own greed and deceit. His carefully constructed façade was crumbling.

Walt, determined to regain control of the narrative, sent video recordings to all major TV channels, attempting to salvage his reputation. In the recordings, he expressed regret for the previous day's incident, claiming he had been unaware of the boy's identity and alleging that the boy was trying to tarnish his reputation. He promised to provide transparency by publicly disclosing his personal secretary's records of transactions, offerings, and donations received and sent to orphanages and old-age homes.

Maxson, however, was not convinced of Walt's innocence. He gathered information about Walt's personal secretary, including his address, wife, and children. He then followed the secretary's only son as he rode his bicycle to school and kidnapped him, taking him to his own room.

When the secretary realized his son was missing, he frantically contacted the school. The school authorities informed him that the boy had left school and was heading home, but they had no further information. The secretary, panic-stricken, desperately sought answers.

Maxson had the kidnapped boy call his father, revealing the abduction. The secretary, distraught and desperate to save his son, agreed to Maxson's demands. Maxson told him to review the reports and transactions, which would expose to the public that Walt had transferred the majority of the donated money to his personal account, leaving only a small portion for the orphanage. The secretary was hesitant, fearing for his life if he exposed Walt's wrongdoings.

Maxson reminded him that he had agreed to exchange his life for his son's. The secretary, cornered and desperate, reluctantly agreed to Maxson's plan. He would publicly reveal Walt's fraudulent activities, shattering the philanthropist's carefully constructed façade.

Chapter-16

The audience anxiously anticipated the secretary's disclosure of Walt's actual character the following day, wondering if he was a good philanthropist or a villain lying behind a show of compassion.

When the secretary revealed Walt's bank account transactions, it became evident that he had misappropriated a significant amount of money donated and raised from the public and kind individuals. The public was horrified to learn of Walt's actual intentions after looking through the transaction records and costs associated with the purported orphanages.

As it turned out, Walt was taking advantage of trusts, old-age homes, and orphanages in order to avoid paying taxes and embezzle public funds. These facilities lacked the required care, sufficient food, and suitable housing. The facilities also suffered from poor maintenance. Walt was far from altruistic, but he had skillfully created the impression of generosity.

When the public learned of this, they erupted in rage and criticism of Walt. As a result, the government had to swiftly investigate the financial transactions and request Walt to provide transparency regarding his income and tax history.

Walt's once impeccable reputation shattered, revealing the dishonest man underneath. After years of meticulous work, Walt's misdeeds irreversibly eroded the public's confidence, ostracizing him and making him pay for his actions.

The throng withdrew after the secretary's scathing exposé, leaving the secretary by himself with Maxson. The secretary asked Maxson to give his son back as the last of the daylight faded, since he had kept his half of the agreement. Recognizing what the secretary had done, Maxson pointed him in the direction of a designated spot for the conversation.

The assigned location was a busy intersection that was brimming with early-morning traffic. The secretary awaited Maxson's return with a mixture of excitement and unease. A little while later, Maxson and secretary's son emerged from the shadows. Maxson gave the youngster over with a somber expression on his face, his eyes sending a quiet message to the secretary.

"Can we speak in private, Mr. Loyal Secretary?" With a foreboding tone in his voice, Maxson questioned Sensing Maxson's plan, the secretary took a while to decide but finally consented. He ensured his son's safe return by sending him home.

Maxson turned to face the secretary and fixed him with an unrelenting gaze as the boy vanished into the distance. "I had stated that I require a trade of your life in order to free your son," Maxson replied, his voice resonating through the darkness. "I fulfilled my share. It's your time now.

Maxson made a quick move and stabbed the secretary in the chest. The secretary noticed a stain of crimson spreading across his shirt, and his eyes widened in shock. A stab of pain surged through his body, but he said nothing, his eyes meeting Maxson's.

Maxson stood there and watched the secretary's life fade away. The secretary's body went limp, and his breathing became shallow. He let out one last breath before his lifeless body collapsed to the floor, the victim of Maxson's cruel game.

Maxson vanished into the night without turning around, leaving the secretary lying in the middle of the busy metropolis as a mute reminder of the depths of human evil. Ignorant to the horror that had occurred right in front of their eyes, the morning traffic rushed around the lifeless body. A cold, planned act of retaliation had destroyed the secretary's life, which had once been full of honor and integrity. The secretary's life had left a trail of unanswered questions and a chilling reminder of the darkness that exists within human hearts.

With the rising of the morning sun, word of the secretary's passing quickly went viral. A group of people congregated near the corpse, their expressions filled with astonishment and incredulity. Constantly on the lookout, the journalists flocked to the scene, their cameras catching every graphic detail. The photographs, plastered over newspaper front pages and carried on radio and television, fueled the public's rising hostility towards Walt.

News anchors portrayed Walt as a monster on television, a merciless individual who could silence anyone who tried to question his well-crafted facade of goodness. Walt's charitable deeds had once won the public over, but now they see him as a phony who has concealed his actual nature behind wealth and power.

Protests broke out in the streets as enraged citizens demanded that authorities take Walt into custody and charge him with a crime. They carried signs with messages such as "Justice for the Secretary" and "Walt, the Wolf in Sheep's Clothing." Outrage spread throughout the city, and people began to demand answers from the man they had previously looked up to.

Stuck in the middle of the storm, the police found themselves in a precarious situation. Walt was a difficult target because of his enormous money and political connections. They were terrified of upsetting such a strong person, even though they had no hard proof connecting him to the secretary's death.

Meanwhile, Walt remained confined to his estate, with his once-immaculate reputation irreparably damaged. The media coverage, demonstrations, and increasing public scrutiny were all part of a coordinated attack against his well-maintained public persona. He realized that the public had irreversibly lost the confidence they had formerly gained so readily.

Walt broke his word and released a deadly gas over his orphanage, killing countless innocent people out of sheer despair and rage. Through the unrelenting media, word of this horrifying deed quickly spread, reaching every part of the country. Walt appeared on live television, his look a mixture of anger and sadness, facing public scrutiny and allegations.

Walt acknowledged his innocence while expressing his sorrow for the catastrophe. Then he switched the blame, accusing Maxson and asserting that he had indisputable proof. Using pictures of Maxson's father, he twisted the truth to connect him to the latest attack on the orphanage and a string of unsolved murders.

According to Walt, Maxson's father was motivated by a dark desire to take the lives of innocent people, portraying him as a cunning man. He said that Maxson was his father's pawn, tricked into committing these horrible deeds by his psychologically damaged history.

Walt left the people confused and uneasy with his passionate plea, which was peppered with well-constructed lies. There was a great deal of mistrust and distrust as a result of the public's diminished faith in both Walt and Maxson.

Walt declared that he had clean hands and that he would tell the truth the next day, as the country held its collective breath. But all he was doing with his statements was trying desperately to restore his damaged reputation.

The public was still split, not knowing who to believe: the unhappy son looking for revenge or the once-loved philanthropist. Walt's image and the orphanage's future were in jeopardy as the lines between truth and deceit became hazy.

Steeped in the searing sting of betrayal, Axel found himself confined to a detention cell, his mind unceasingly reliving the sequence of events that had brought him to his knees. An unquenchable need for vengeance raged in his heart, and he yearned to take his anger out on Maxson, the man he had previously regarded as a faithful friend.

Axel's ideas of revenge were racing through his mind when the warden's voice announced that a guest had arrived. Presuming it was Maxson, Axel steeled himself for a confrontation he really wanted to avoid. Curtly responding to the warden, "I don't want to see anyone,"

But the warden's harsh look and commanding voice said otherwise. "You have to meet them, whether you like it or not," he maintained. Axel reluctantly moved into the waiting room, doubt and distrust racing through his head.

Axel was shocked to see Walt, the person Maxson had vowed to destroy, approaching the guest. Walt held out a hand in greeting, his charm and manner ever so unique. Walt said, "I know Maxson has betrayed you," his words echoing Axel's own suffering.

Surprised by Walt's candor, Axel could only nod in agreement. Walt's remarks resonated deeply with him, as the wounds from betrayal were still fresh. "What if I could help your exact revenge on Maxson?" Walt went on, his tone slightly inclined toward persuasion. "I can even secure your release from this prison if you're willing to join me and follow my instructions."

Axel's fervent desire for retribution drew him to Walt's offer. He was filled with hope at the idea of exacting revenge for Maxson's betrayal. Axel admitted with a shaky voice that he had sacrificed so much for Maxson, only to be betrayed by his selfish motives. "I yearn for nothing more than to make him pay for his deceit."

Walt smiled mischievously, knowing Axel's weakness and need for retribution. He had discovered the ideal pawn in his rivalry with Maxson. With Axel under his control, Walt was convinced that triumph was within his grasp.

After arranging for Axel's release from prison, Walt and Axel emerged from the walls, ready to collaborate and confront Maxson. Axel heard Walt's orders clearly and resolved to carry them out.

The next day, Axel found himself in the spotlight, appearing live on one of Walt's television stations. The media and the public eagerly anticipated his statements, trying to discover the truth behind the recent occurrences.

With a confident posture, Axel began his presentation by saying, "I understand the confusion that has clouded your minds in recent days. I am coming to uncover the truth, a revelation that will expose Maxson for the deceitful and terrible man he truly is."

Axel's voice resonated with conviction as he delved into Maxson's past, exposing a horrific narrative of selfishness and brutality. "Maxson is not the man you think he is," Axel asserted. "He has a dark history-a trail of ruin and murder left in his wake. I know him better than anyone, having been his friend since college."

Axel's statements sent shockwaves through the audience, their perception of Maxson collapsing before their eyes. Axel painted a portrait of a man driven by vengeance, consumed by his father's wicked intentions.

Axel admitted, with a trace of shame coloring his tone, that he had been blinded by their friendship and failed to see the darkness lurking within Maxson. "Mr. Walt, a man of noble intentions and genuine concern for society, has enlightened me," Axel said, a trace of shame coloring his tone.

Axel's admission moved the spotlight to Walt, portraying him in a favorable light. He portrayed Walt as a victim of Maxson's intrigues, a man falsely condemned and unfairly mistreated.

"I made a grave mistake in aligning myself with Maxson against Mr. Walt," Axel acknowledged, his voice filled with guilt. "Maxson manipulated me, using me as a pawn in his twisted game."

Axel then dove into the reality of the orphanage incident, uncovering Maxson's role in the tragedy. Axel revealed that Maxson, not Walt, masterminded the toxic gas assault, driven by a need for vengeance against Walt.

"Maxson's father was a cold-blooded killer, responsible for the deaths of innocent children," Axel admitted, his voice husky with passion. "Maxson, following in his father's footsteps, has shown no remorse for his actions, even resorting to murder to achieve his goals."

Axel's statements painted a horrifying picture of Maxson, a man consumed by an insatiable desire for devastation and chaos. He asked the people to understand Maxson for who he truly was-a dangerous and manipulative individual who constituted a threat to society.

In conclusion, Axel urged the public, "We must stand together against Maxson's terrible designs. He is a psychological menace, a man who thrives on chaos and ruin. We must expel him from our society before it's too late."

With a final nod of gratitude to Walt, Axel completed his address, leaving the crowd startled and shaken. His remarks had exposed the truth, revealing Maxson's true nature and the innocence of Walt. The public was forced to cope with the consequences of Axel's revelations; their opinion of Walt and Maxson was forever transformed.

Chapter-17

As Maxson listened to his dearest friend Axel's impassioned speech, he felt a wave of despair wash over him. Axel portrayed Walt as a noble savior, while Maxson as a heartless monster. Maxson realized that Axel's rhetoric had swayed the people, causing his he art to sink.

Unable to bear the weight of the crowd's judgment, Maxson wandered aimlessly through the streets. As he walked, a barrage of hostility met him. People whispered behind his back; their voices laced with disgust. Others openly condemned him, their words like daggers piercing his heart. Some even spat at him, their contempt palpable. And then there were those who hurled stones at him, their anger boiling over into violence.

Maxson felt a wave of shame and humiliation wash over him. He had always considered himself a good man, but now he was being treated as if he were the scum of the earth. He couldn't understand how people could be so quick to judge him without even knowing the truth.

Despite the pain and humiliation, Maxson refused to give up. He knew that he was innocent, and he was determined to prove it. But how could he clear his name when everyone had already made up their minds?

As Maxson continued to walk, he overheard snippets of conversations from passersby. They were all talking about him, and their words were filled with hatred and disgust. "How could he do such a thing?" one woman exclaimed. "He's a monster!" another man declared.

Maxson's heart sank even further. The people's words were like poison, slowly seeping into his soul. He felt like he was drowning in a sea of despair.

But then he remembered something that Axel had said in his speech. Axel had said that Maxson was a powerful sorcerer, capable of great evil. But Axel had also said that Maxson was a coward, too afraid to use his power for good.

Consumed by rage and despair, Maxson found himself paralyzed, unable to take any action. Walt's ominous prophecy echoed in his mind, "You will lose everything and be left helpless." And now, Walt's words have rung true. Maxson had lost everything that was dear to him: his father, his brother, his sister, and even his closest friend, Axel.

Axel, once a confidant and ally, now despised Maxson, his respect and loyalty replaced by contempt and hatred. The weight of public condemnation crushed Maxson's spirit. People ostracized, shunned, and blamed him for crimes he didn't commit. Loneliness gnawed at him, and despair threatened to consume him.

Penniless and without hope, Maxson contemplated the unthinkable-ending his own life. Walt had won, holding all the cards, leaving Maxson with nothing but an empty hand and a shattered soul. The game was Walt's to play, and Maxson was a mere pawn in his twisted scheme.

Consumed by despair, Maxson succumbed to the belief that defeating Walt was an insurmountable task. Walt's position of power and influence, his wealth, political connections, and public adoration seemed insurmountable. Maxson felt like a mere pawn in Walt's grand scheme, a disposable piece in a game he could never win.

Overwhelmed by the weight of his failures and the humiliation he had endured, Maxson found himself in a desolate children's park, his spirit crushed. As he contemplated ending his life, a letter from his brother slipped from his pocket. The words of his beloved brother echoed in his mind: "You are our last hope. Please don't disappoint us. Our father failed, and I failed. We are counting on you."

The letter rekindled a spark of hope within Maxson's shattered soul. He couldn't let his family down; he couldn't give up on them. As he wiped away his tears and steeled his resolve, a voice broke through his despair.

"Maxson, I will help you," a young girl declared.

Maxson turned to face the unexpected savior, a young girl of no more than fifteen, her eyes filled with determination. She disclosed that she was one of the girls rescued from Walt's orphanage. The horrors she had witnessed and endured fueled her desire to bring Walt to justice.

Maxson's heart flickered with a renewed sense of purpose. This young girl, with her unwavering spirit and firsthand knowledge of Walt's atrocities, could be the key to his downfall. Together, they could expose Walt's true nature and bring him to justice.

Empowered by this newfound alliance, Maxson emerged from the depths of despair, ready to confront Walt and reclaim his life. The path ahead would be arduous, but Maxson was no longer alone. He had found a kindred spirit, a beacon of hope in his darkest hour.

With a glimmer of hope rekindled in his eyes, Maxson listened intently as the young girl revealed the atrocities she had witnessed at Walt's orphanage. "I know everything that happens there," she declared, her voice trembling with emotion. "The illegal experiments, the inhuman treatment, the abuse... I've seen it all."

Since being forced into the orphanage as a child, she endured a series of horrors. The children were regularly subjected to the release of poisonous hydrogen cyanide gas to sedate them, forced labor, and medical experiments performed without their consent.

"I've heard Walt's evil plans," she continued, her voice laced with determination. "I know what he's capable of. And I won't let him get away with it anymore."

Maxson's heart swelled with gratitude for the girl's courage and resilience. She was a beacon of hope, a testament to the indomitable human spirit.

"But we need proof," Maxson interjected, his mind racing with the challenges ahead. "Without evidence, our words will fall on deaf ears."

The girl nodded in understanding. "I know," she said. "But I'm not afraid. I'll go back to the orphanage and gather the evidence we need."

Maxson's eyes widened in surprise. "You're willing to risk your life?"

"I have nothing left to lose. And I'll do everything in my power to help you."

The girl's selflessness deeply moved Maxson. He knew that her mission was fraught with danger, but he also knew that she was the only one who could infiltrate the orphanage and uncover the truth.

With a heavy heart, he handed her his mobile phone. "Call me as soon as you have the evidence," he instructed. "I'll be waiting."

The girl nodded and turned to leave, her small frame disappearing into the shadows. Maxson watched her go, a surge of determination coursing through his veins. He would not let her down.

The girl slipped back into the orphanage, her heart pounding with a mixture of fear and determination. She had been absent for a week, and her absence had not escaped notice. The staff members questioned her about her whereabouts, but she feigned amnesia, claiming to have no recollection of the previous week.

Her excuse seemed to satisfy them, and no one pressed her further. They were relieved to have her back, for she was one of the few diligent and dependable girls in the orphanage.

That day, Walt was in a state of drunken stupor, his mind clouded by drugs. He vented his frustrations on the staff, lashing out with verbal and physical abuse. In a fit of rage, he lit a cigarette and dialed a number on his phone.

"How will you pay for...?" he slurred; his voice thick with intoxication. "No, that's not fair."

His eyes fell upon a young girl, her face streaked with tears. Without a second thought, he grabbed her arm and pulled her towards him.

"Sweetie," he croaked, his voice dripping with sarcasm, "you're in luck. Tomorrow, a life of luxury awaits you. A rich family is eager to have you as their personal assistant to clean, cook, and run errands. Aren't you excited?"

The girl remained silent, her tears flowing freely. Walt, unfazed by her lack of enthusiasm, dismissed her with a wave of his hand.

"Get her ready for tomorrow's trade," he instructed a nearby staff member, his voice laced with disdain.

The staff members exchanged sorrowful glances; their hearts heavy with pity for the girl's fate. Little did they know, the girl sent by Maxson was discreetly capturing their every move. She discreetly recorded the entire exchange, her heart pounding with a mix of anger and determination.

As the day drew to a close, the girl stealthily gathered evidence of the orphanage's deplorable conditions. She snapped photos of the poor-quality infrastructure, the meager and unhygienic food, and the scars etched on the children's bodies-silent testimonies to the torture they had endured.

With a heavy heart, she managed to convince a sympathetic staff member to provide a video recording of Walt's cruelty. Armed with this damning evidence, she slipped out of the orphanage, her mission accomplished.

She rushed to Maxson, her hands trembling as she handed him the phone, the memory card, and the photos. Maxson watched the videos and examined the photos, his eyes widening in disbelief and outrage.

The evidence was undeniable-a stark revelation of Walt's sinister intentions and the inhumane treatment he subjected the children to. With this newfound weapon, Maxson knew that Walt's reign of terror was coming to an end.

Chapter-18

Maxson expressed his deepest gratitude to the girl for her bravery and selflessness. He acknowledged that her intervention had saved his life, preventing him from succumbing to his suicidal thoughts. "Without you," he confessed, "I would have been lost, a hopeless wanderer with no direction. Thank you for everything you've done for me-for your unwavering support, your sacrifices, and the risks you've taken. It won't be long now before we can put an end to Walt's reign of terror."

With a renewed sense of purpose, Maxson and the girl recorded a video message and sent it to every major television channel and media outlet. During peak viewing hours the next day, every major television channel and media outlet broadcasted Maxson's message across the nation. With a calm but determined demeanor, he addressed the public:

"Hello everyone. I'm making this recording to reach out to three people in particular. First, I have a message for Walt, then for my dear friend Axel, and finally, for the public at large.

Walt, I'm speaking to you directly. Your reign of terror ends today. We will no longer tolerate your manipulation, threats, and violence. You have caused enough pain and suffering. It's time for you to face the consequences of your actions.

Axel, my friend, I know you're out there, and I want you to know that I'm not giving up on you. I believe in you, and I know that you can overcome this. Don't let Walt control you any longer. Find your own strength and stand up for what's right.

And finally, to the public, I urge you to speak up and stand against injustice. Don't let fear silence your voice. Together, we can make a difference. Together, let's create a world where we treat everyone with respect and dignity.

Maxson's message to Walt was a chilling declaration of intent. With a voice laced with determination, he laid down the gauntlet:

"Walt, this is an open challenge to you. Your time is up. You will face your death at my hands. If you have the courage, face me like a man.

Your evil deeds will not go unpunished. The public will know the truth about your atrocities, your inhumanity, and your true nature. The public will expose you for the monster you are.

We will settle this matter privately, but mark my words, your death is inevitable. Tomorrow, you will meet your end."

Turning his attention to Axel, Maxson's tone softened, replaced by a deep remorse. "Axel, my dearest friend, words cannot express my profound regret for my betrayal. You stood by me through thick and thin, until the very end, when I turned my back on you. I know my actions were unforgivable, a stain that will forever mar our friendship.

Please hear my plea. I was manipulated, threatened, and blackmailed by Walt. He held my father's reputation hostage, threatening to destroy him and innocent children if I didn't betray you. He even framed us for the crime, ensuring our imprisonment.

Even after you were sent to jail, Walt broke his promise and continued to deceive us. He was the one who orchestrated your imprisonment and then feigned your release, only to turn you against me.

I never stopped hoping for our friendship, Axel. I will always cherish the bond we shared, and I will welcome you with open arms if you ever wish to see me again."

With a heavy heart, Maxson turned his attention to the public, addressing their collective innocence and susceptibility to manipulation. "Dear people, I pity your naivety. You blindly accept what you hear and see, failing to question the underlying causes and motives. You've been conditioned like puppets, dancing to the tune of those who hold power over you.

My father, a beacon of hope, sought to eradicate social imbalance and injustice, but his quest ended in tragedy. Yet, you remain trapped in the shackles of hierarchy, elevating those with wealth and influence above those with compassion and humanity.

The rich prosper by exploiting the poor, perpetuating a cycle of inequality. You revere those who hold greater power and influence, neglecting those in need of your assistance and respect. Instead, you seek approval from those you perceive as superior, only to be met with disrespect and flattery towards those above them.

This self-perpetuating cycle of servitude is robbing you of your purpose and dignity. We must eradicate hierarchy, which acts like a cancer. Your actions, driven by a thirst for attention and superficial gain, are meaningless and ultimately harmful to yourselves and others.

It is time to awaken from your slumber, to break free from the chains of manipulation, and to embrace the truth. You have the power to change the world and create a society where justice, equality, and compassion reign supreme. Stand up for what is right for those who are oppressed and marginalized.

We can work together to dismantle hierarchical structures and create a world that values and respects every individual. Let us reclaim our lives, our voices, and our potential. The future lies in our hands, not in the hands of those who seek to control us."

"Your actions reveal a profound lack of understanding about the consequences of your choices. You fail to discern who truly deserves your generosity and compassion, often squandering your resources on those who have no need for them.

In a lavish hotel, you overpay the waiter, indulging in an act of conspicuous generosity that does little to address the underlying issues of inequality. Yet, when confronted with a street vendor or a farmer, you haggle and negotiate relentlessly, driving down their prices to a pittance.

This injustice is glaring. The farmer and the street vendor are the ones who truly need that money to survive, not the waiter in a luxurious establishment. Why do you treat them with such indifference? Why do you willingly give to those who don't need it while begrudging every cent to those who desperately struggle to make ends meet?

Your actions are driven by a superficial desire for prestige, an illusion of superiority that blinds you to the true meaning of compassion. You lack the courage to confront a thief armed with a knife, but you have no qualms about intimidating a poor child stealing out of hunger or chastising a beggar seeking alms.

This distorted perception of reality has been carefully cultivated, shaping your behavior and obscuring your moral compass. Walt has been exploiting this vulnerability, trafficking innocent children into servitude for the wealthy.

These so-called 'elite' individuals, already brimming with wealth and privilege, refuse to pay fair wages for domestic labor. Instead, they seek to control and exploit these vulnerable children, feeding their own greed at the expense of their victims' innocence and well-being.

Their hearts are as barren as their actions. They may possess material wealth, but they lack the compassion and humanity that define true wealth.

Your choices have consequences. They perpetuate a system of inequality and injustice where the rich grow richer by exploiting the poor and the vulnerable.

It is time to break free from this cycle of exploitation. Recognize the true value of compassion and generosity, and direct your kindness towards those who truly need it.

Stand up for the rights of the marginalized, the voiceless, and the exploited. Challenge the structures of power that perpetuate inequality and demand a society where justice and fairness prevail."

Maxson's Message to the Public

Dear People,

I am here to expose the true nature of Walt, the man you believe to be a pillar of generosity and benevolence. His facade of kindness is nothing more than a mask that conceals a heart of darkness and a soul devoid of compassion.

Walt has been exploiting the generosity of the public and the trust of those who believe in his charitable endeavors. He has diverted funds intended for the well being of orphans to his own personal gain, leaving the children under his care to suffer in squalid conditions and lacking essential necessities.

The photograph below depicts the deplorable state of the orphanage that Walt claims to operate. The children are cramped into overcrowded rooms, the water is contaminated, and the food is barely edible. These conditions are a far cry from the idyllic image that Walt has carefully crafted for himself.

The video below, taken from inside the orphanage, reveals Walt in his true form. He is seen engaging in a drug-fueled conversation about the trafficking of children, further exposing his depravity and disregard for the well-being of the most vulnerable members of our society.

[Video of Walt engaging in a drug-fueled conversation about the trafficking of children]

Walt has deceived you for far too long. His acts of philanthropy are nothing more than a charade to mask his true intentions. He masquerades as a benefactor, exploiting the generosity of others to fulfill his sinister cravings.

It is time to awaken from your slumber and recognize the truth about Walt. Do not be fooled by his façade of generosity; he is a predator who has exploited your trust for his own selfish gain.

Join me in exposing Walt's true nature and demanding justice for the victims of his exploitation. Together, we can create a society where compassion and benevolence prevail, and where the most vulnerable are not left to suffer at the hands of those who claim to care.

Walt's legacy will not be one of generosity and benevolence but one of deceit, exploitation, and cruelty. He has left a trail of pain and suffering in his wake, and his actions have shattered the lives of countless individuals.

However, his legacy does not define us. We can choose a different path, guided by compassion, integrity, and justice. By standing up for what is right and creating a world where every individual is treated with dignity and respect, we can honor the victims of Walt's exploitation.

Together, we can build a legacy of hope and change, a legacy that will truly reflect the values of kindness and compassion. Let us not allow Walt's darkness to consume us; let us instead shine a light of truth and justice that will illuminate a brighter future for all.

Recordings of the Staff Member on the Orphanage

"I have worked here for many years as a staff member, caring for the children under Walt's supervision. We endured deplorable conditions. The company did not pay us fairly, and they constantly threatened to fire us if we spoke out against the injustices taking place.

Walt was a man consumed by drugs and abuse. He regularly mistreated both the staff and the children under his care. His actions were driven by a single-minded pursuit of wealth and power, and he had no qualms about exploiting the vulnerable to achieve his goals.

Walt's primary source of income was not the orphanage but rather the illegal trafficking of children. He sold girls into servitude in wealthy households and forced boys into grueling labor, such as construction and farm work.

The children under his care were treated as mere commodities, their well-being and happiness of no concern to him. He saw them as nothing more than tools to be used for his own personal gain."

Maxson's Final Statement

"One more truth must be revealed: my father is innocent of the crimes he was accused of. The truth will come out when Walt's murder takes place tomorrow."

With this final statement, the recordings came to an end. The public was left reeling from the shocking revelations, their trust in Walt shattered, and their hearts filled with anger and sorrow for the victims of his exploitation.

Chapter-19

"As Walt watched the recordings on the television screen, a sense of liberation washed over him. He had meticulously crafted a façade of being a good man, but now he was done pretending. The wealth he had amassed through his unscrupulous dealings, he mused, would sustain him for generations to come. He was weary of the charade of running trusts, orphanages, and old-age homes. The public, he knew, was well aware of his true nature. Yet a flicker of rage still burned in Walt's eyes. Maxson, that insolent whelp, had dared to expose his true self, believing he had shattered Walt's carefully constructed image. But Walt cared little about public perception. He had only one desire: to eliminate Maxson.

Maxson, in his naivety, believed he had destroyed Walt's reputation. But he was unaware of the depths of Walt's ruthlessness. Only Maxson's father, now deceased, had fully grasped Walt's capacity for violence. Maxson, the last remaining offspring of his former friend, had unwittingly crossed a dangerous line. Consumed by an insatiable thirst for vengeance, Walt cared nothing for public opinion. He had vowed to silence Maxson with his own hands to sever the final tie to his past.

'Let the world see who emerges victorious,' Walt thought grimly. He needed no accomplices, no backup. His bare hands were more than enough to extinguish that young man's breath. Walt, consumed by an insatiable hunger for revenge, ordered his men to surveil the city, searching for Maxson. He would eliminate this obstacle, the last vestige of his friend's family, and finally achieve peace."

Maxson and the girl sat on a swing in the deserted children's park, the shadows of dusk deepening around them. The girl's voice, laced with worry, broke the silence. "Maxson," she asked, "how are we going to kill him?"

Maxson sighed, his gaze fixed on the empty playground. "I don't know," he confessed. "Walt is a cunning man. He knows he can defeat me alone, so he won't bring any backup. It's a one-on-one battle, and only one of us will walk out alive."

His voice hardened, a steely resolve replacing the uncertainty. "I know it's difficult to accept, but I've had to take lives before," he continued, his eyes burning with determination. "And defeating Walt will be as hard, if not harder. He's a man of sixty, but he's still formidable-trickle, strong, and fearless."

He turned to the girl, his expression softening. "That's why I'm asking you to stay away from me during the fight. It's going to take place in this park at midnight. There won't be anyone else here. You, Walt, and I Please find a hiding spot and watch. If I win, we'll leave together. But if Walt wins, please, I beg of you, find a way to escape. If he discovers you're here, he'll kill you without hesitation."

His voice dropped to a low whisper, laced with desperation. "Let's hope for the best and wait," he concluded, his eyes scanning the darkening landscape.

Meanwhile, the spies dispatched by Walt had located Maxson's whereabouts and relayed the information back to their master. Walt, upon hearing the news, let out a grim grin. "It's time to settle this," he muttered to himself, a sense of anticipation coursing through his veins.

As the clock struck midnight, the deserted children's park lay shrouded in an eerie silence. The moon, casting an ethereal glow upon the empty swings and slides, seemed to hold its breath in anticipation of the impending confrontation.

Maxson, his heart pounding with a mixture of fear and determination, sat tensely on a weathered bench, his eyes scanning the darkness for any sign of his adversary. The girl, her face pale and drawn with anxiety, had concealed herself beneath a nearby slide, her eyes wide with fear as she watched the park's entrance through the narrow gap.

The silence was shattered by the crunch of tires on gravel. A car materialized out of the shadows, its headlights cutting through the darkness like twin daggers. The car skidded to a halt, and Walt, his face grim and determined, stepped out.

With a heavy tread, Walt approached Maxson, his eyes burning with an intensity that sent shivers down the younger man's spine. He stopped directly in front of the bench, his towering figure casting a menacing shadow over Maxson.

"I am sorry to say to my deceased friend," Walt began, his voice dripping with venom, "that his entire family will be destroyed and his era will end. If you meet your father after death, please convey this message from me."

A chilling smile played on Walt's lips, a stark contrast to the fury that raged within his eyes. In a swift and unexpected move, he lashed out with a kick, his foot connecting with Maxson's chest with a sickening thud.

Maxson, caught off guard by the sudden attack, stumbled backward, his back slamming against the bench. Walt, relishing the moment, pressed his foot down on Maxson's chest, savoring the feeling of power it gave him.

But fueled by a surge of adrenaline, Maxson refused to surrender easily. With a burst of strength, he heaved Walt's leg off his chest and shoved him away. Walt, caught off guard by Maxson's unexpected resistance, struggled to regain his balance.

In a blink of an eye, Maxson was on his feet, his eyes blazing with a newfound intensity. Walt, realizing that he had underestimated his opponent, braced himself for the inevitable clash.

Two men's fate would be decided in a battle that would echo through the deserted children's park long after the moon had set.

As the two figures clashed under the moonlight, the children's park became a battleground, their movements a blur of fists and fury. Walt, with his years of experience and raw strength, pressed the attack, his blows raining down upon Maxson like a relentless storm. Maxson, though bloodied and bruised, fought back with a tenacity that belied his injuries. His movements, fueled by a mix of rage and determination, were unpredictable and fierce.

The fight raged on for what seemed like an eternity, each man refusing to yield. Maxson, his face battered and his breath coming in ragged gasps, fought with every ounce of strength he possessed. Walt, though tiring, remained relentless, his determination to end this once and for all fueling his every move.

As the minutes stretched into hours, the battle began to take its toll on both men. Maxson's movements grew slower, and his body was battered and bruised. Walt, too, was weary, his once-pristine suit now stained with blood and dirt. But neither man would back down.

Finally, with a surge of adrenaline, Maxson landed a blow that sent Walt reeling backward. Walt stumbled; his eyes wide with shock. Maxson, sensing his opponent's vulnerability, pressed his advantage, launching a flurry of punches that forced Walt further off balance.

Walt, desperate to regain control of the fight, grabbed Maxson around the throat, his grip tightening with every passing moment. Maxson, his vision blurring, gasped for air, his body struggling against Walt's suffocating grip.

As Maxson's consciousness began to fade, his thoughts turned to his brother, Merrick. Regret washed over him as he realized he had failed to avenge his death. "Merrick, forgive me," he whispered, his voice barely audible. "I tried... I really did..."

With his last remaining strength, Maxson's vision darkened, and he slumped to the ground, his body lifeless.

Walt, his chest heaving, released his grip, his eyes filled with a mixture of triumph and relief.

The children's park, once a place of laughter and joy, now bears the scars of a brutal battle. Walt, his clothes torn and bloodied, stood alone amidst the wreckage, a victor but a changed man.

The girl who had been watching the fight between Maxson and Walt felt a knot of fear tighten in her stomach. She knew that if Walt saw her, he would kill her without hesitation. She had to stay hidden, but her heart ached at the thought of watching her friend die in front of her eyes.

She glanced around the park, her eyes darting from shadow to shadow. Suddenly, she spotted a small, brittle stone lying on the ground. An idea sparked in her mind. She picked up the stone, her fingers trembling slightly.

Taking a deep breath, she focused her aim on Walt's head. With all her might, she threw the stone. It whizzed through the air, striking Walt squarely on the forehead. The impact was sickening, and Walt let out a grunt of pain.

His hands loosened their grip on Maxson's neck, and Maxson gasped for air. He coughed and sputtered, his vision blurred but still able to make out Walt's stunned expression.

Fueled by a surge of adrenaline and fury, Maxson scrambled to his feet. He grabbed the stone from the ground and raised it above his head.

With a scream of rage, he brought the stone down on Walt's head, striking him over and over again. Walt's face contorted in pain, and his body slumped to the ground.

Maxson continued to beat Walt until his hands were slick with blood. Walt's skull cracked open, and blood pooled around his lifeless body.

Maxson stood there, panting heavily, his hands trembling. He looked down at Walt, a strange mix of relief and horror washing over him.

"Congratulations," Walt whispered, his voice barely audible. "You've won."

And then Walt's eyes fluttered closed, and his breath stilled.

Maxson closed Walt's eyes with his own hand. He thought of his father, his brother, and his sister. He thought of all the pain and loss he had endured.

As Maxson lay on the ground, his body aching and his spirit weary, he looked up at the sky, which was dotted with countless stars. The girl approached him; her face etched with concern.

"You've won," she said softly, her voice barely a whisper.

Maxson managed a weak smile. "Technically, we've won," he replied. "You saved me for the second time."

The girl kneeled beside him and gently wiped his bloodstained face with a handkerchief. She then offered him some water, which he drank gratefully. As the cool liquid revitalized him, Maxson found the strength to stand up.

He reached into his pocket and pulled out a torn and dusty letter. It was the letter Merrick had received from his father. Maxson placed the letter on Walt's chest and then placed a bloodstained stone on top of it to hold it in place.

With the girl's help, Maxson slowly walked out of the park, leaving Walt's lifeless body behind. They walked in silence; their thoughts consumed by the events of the night.

As they emerged from the park, the first rays of dawn were painting the sky with hues of pink and orange. Maxson turned to the girl and smiled.

"Thank you," he said sincerely. "I don't know what I would have done without you."

The girl nodded, her eyes shining with a newfound determination. "We'll be okay," she said. "We'll get through this together."

The morning sun cast its golden rays upon the children's park, revealing a scene of utter devastation. Walt's lifeless body sprawled on the ground, beneath a heavy stone rested a bloodstained letter.

A crowd had gathered around the scene, their faces etched with a mix of shock and curiosity. The media and police had arrived, eager to unravel the mystery behind the death of the once-respected businessman.

A gasp swept through the crowd as the letter was unearthed and read aloud. Finally, the crowd gasped as the truth, buried beneath layers of deceit, was laid bare. Walt, portrayed as a hero, was actually a ruthless manipulator, a pawn in a much larger game.

Maxson's father penned the letter, revealing the sordid tale of Walt's treachery. It detailed how Walt had conspired with powerful individuals to frame Maxson's father for crimes he did not commit. The letter also exposed Walt's involvement in the death of Maxson's brother, Merrick.

The revelation sent shockwaves through the community, shattering the carefully constructed façade that Walt had maintained for years. The media, once quick to praise Walt, now turned on him, their headlines screaming with tales of his betrayal.

The police, armed with the truth, launched a full-scale investigation into Walt's crimes. They discovered a trail of evidence that linked Walt to a series of illegal activities, including corruption, money laundering, and even murder.

Walt's empire crumbled around him as his allies abandoned him, their trust shattered by his deceit. His deceit shattered their trust, leaving him alone as a pariah in the world he had once ruled.

Finally, Maxson, the man who had been wronged and vilified, received exoneration. They cleared his father's name and revealed the truth about his brother's death.

The children's park, once a place of joy and laughter, had become a symbol of justice and redemption. The morning sun, shining upon the scene, seemed to herald a new dawn, a time of truth and accountability.

A letter being read on TV

As the crowd dispersed, the children's park stood empty, silently reminding everyone of the events that had transpired within its walls.

❞

Letter to Merrick

To Merrick,

This is the letter of my last wishes, my precious son. I want to apologize for not being a good father to you and our family. I know it is not what I want to do, but I should. We live in an unfair world, and I have been fighting against the law since I was a young child: "The voices of those who are higher in the hierarchy and have money and power are heard, but the voices of ordinary and poor people are not considered." Hierarchy should exist in architecture and design, not in the lives of people who are based on money and authority. I hadn't shared my early years with you. When I was fifteen years old, our entire village was suffering from a drought and extreme poverty. We had no food to survive, and elderly people and small children were dying from starvation. Eventually, a group of people arrived in our village and offered to provide food for a child between the ages of ten and fifteen in exchange for labor in a cold mine. They accepted my offer to go there, and I did.

I had been working there for almost three months, along with many other children my age who were working twelve hours a day only to survive the drought. One day, a caravan arrived and transported me and another boy from the mine to a wealthy home, where we became servants responsible for household chores and gardening, receiving very little money in return. We now understand that we were traded from the mine to assist these individuals. We both felt disappointed and believed that our lives were not meant to unfold in this manner. In order to ensure their safety, other kids are also working on mines for trading. After he identified himself as a Rhode, we developed a close bond.

We both decided to inform society about the reality of child trafficking for financial gain and labor. We successfully escaped the house and reported this to the authorities. However, they didn't want to hear that at all. We learned that a child had died in a mine, leading us to believe that it may have been a murder. We were there to provide evidence of witnesses who had worked on mines, but they wouldn't listen to our response that "the law of hierarchy repeats." We became enraged and made the decision that we should acquire power and wealth and carry out justice on our own if the world only wants to hear the opinions of those with these attributes. We both agreed, stole the money, and plundered the jewelry and small businesses. We both completed our education at a prison school and were subsequently released upon turning eighteen. "The law of hierarchy repeats" is what we said at our march against crimes and injustices in society, but no one paid attention. We have established our own trust and amassed some money thanks to kind donations. In order to end child labor and provide for the needs of the orphaned children, we began to operate orphanages.

After facing numerous challenges from politicians, government officials, and non-governmental organizations that opposed us, we made the decision to kill people in order to obtain money, even if it meant performing some kind and honorable things. We began executing those who opposed us one by one. We have a man in place to take out all of our threats in less than a night. We exchanged our faith for numerous donations. However, as time went on, I witnessed Rhodes's vile and avaricious face. He began stealing money from the donations to meet his own expenses. I cautioned him against doing this since we have a purpose and, given our upbringing, we ought to assist people in need. Rhode feigned acceptance, but he wasn't. Rhode instructed me to disperse the illegally purchased hydrogen cyanide across the building where our adversaries were being housed, intending to kill them. However, I eventually learned that the youngsters who had just joined the orphanage were not enemies. I just put on a blindfold and trusted Rhode, despite my extreme humiliation and guilt about what I had done. A few youngsters passed away, some of them from the effects of the gas. Rhode intended to solicit donations from the public in order to line his own pockets with the proceeds from the deaths of those helpless children.

Above all, he committed the most heinous act: he began exchanging kid labor for wealthy people at cheap salaries. We had made the decision to end child labor and had set out on our mission, but greed and money clouded his judgment. I had learned of his malevolent face. I became enraged and threatened to tell everyone the truth about him. However, he played first. He presented me to the world as someone who had slain innocent children in order to make money, and people blindly believed him. I was merely a pawn in his hands; he merely exploited and discarded me. I made an effort to tell people the truth, but as the saying goes, "The law of hierarchy repeats; they want to hear from Rhode, who was higher in hierarchy, not from me."

Rhode received money, influence, and political support beyond his wildest dreams. He was a man who put on a nice and pleasant mask. Go find him and kill him; Rhode was not his social name.

He chose a good moment to kill me. I could be killed at any time, so please reveal his genuine identity to the public. Above all, I want you to actively spread the word about abolishing the Law of Hierarchy. Those further up the social hierarchy and possessing wealth and power hear the words, while the voices of common people and the impoverished are not even considered.

But still, people love to follow blind rules and want to play a losing game.